CECE BELL
Color by David Lasky

AMULET BOOKS
NEW YORK

El Deafo

SUPERPOWERED EDITION!

Library of Congress Control Number: 2020934335

ISBN 978-1-4197-4831-8

Text and illustrations copyright © 2020 Cece Bell

Color by David Lasky
Book design by Cece Bell and Kate Fitch
Extra content designed by Cece Bell and Megan Kelchner

The Phonic Ear is the registered trademark of
William Dernant Holding A/S. Used by permission.

Printed and bound in China
10 9 8 7 6 5 4 3 2 1

Amulet Books are available at special discounts when
purchased in quantity for premiums and promotions as
well as fundraising or educational use. Special editions
can also be created to specification. For details, contact
specialsales@abramsbooks.com or the address below.

Amulet Books® is a registered
trademark of Harry N. Abrams, Inc.

ABRAMS The Art of Books
195 Broadway, New York, NY 10007
abramsbooks.com

For George and Barbara Bell,
parents extraordinaire

I was a regular little kid. I played with my mom's stuff.

I watched TV with my big brother, Ashley, and my big sister, Sarah.

♪BatMAN!♪

I rode on the back of my father's bicycle.

WHEEEEEEEEEEEE!

I found caterpillars with my friend Emma.

And I sang.

WE ALL LIVE IN A YELLOW SUBMARINE, A YELLOW SUBMARINE—

But then everything changed.

—A YELLOW SUBMARINE...

CECE?

GEORGE! DO SOMETHING! HURRY!

My parents rush me to the hospital.

2

I am pulled away from my parents...

...and taken to a room. Somebody sticks a needle in my back.

3

I wake up. I'm in a different room.

ONLY

A doctor comes... WE NEED TO MEASURE YOUR HEAD!

...and a nurse comes... THIS WON'T HURT A BIT!

...and oh, but my head hurts. Really bad!

The arm prickings and head measurings are endless! It looks like I'll be here for a while.

But after many days of treatment, I am well enough to share a room with another sick kid.

Something is *different*, though. But *what?* I can't quite figure it out.

CECE. *CECE!* WANT SOME ICE CREAM? HUH—I GUESS SHE DOESN'T WANT ANY...

For one thing, how come I never get any ice cream? The other kid gets it all the time!

Why can't Ashley and Sarah come up to my room to talk to me?

THEY MIGHT HAVE GERMS AND SO THEY CAN'T COME UP...

And how come the TV doesn't make any sense?

Everything is so—*quiet.*

It's not all bad, though. I get lots of great gifts!

And I start to feel better. I put on one of the gifts. It's time to get up!

But I can't stand up—

I think I might even be *all* better!

Finally—*finally!*—I get to leave the hospital...

...and go home.

Miracle of miracles, my siblings are being nice to me!

Ashley has made and hidden hundreds of paper boats all around the house just for me...

...and has filled each one with a special surprise.

CANDY!

And Sarah sits close to my bed at night...

...until I fall asleep.

I wake up every morning happy and relieved to be home.

I stay close to Mama, no matter where she is.

But suddenly, I lose her.

11

Where is she?

I call out but she doesn't answer me!

When I finally find her, I know that everything is different. I think she knows it, too.

I CAN'T HEAR...

two

It's been two weeks since the hospital. Just because I can't hear good doesn't mean I can't *look* good.

I *love* my bathing suit.

I wear it—and nothing else—

every day, everywhere.

I LOOK *FANTASTIC!*

But today, it looks like I have to get "dressed."

I don't want to!

But I do.

WE MUST BE GOING SOMEWHERE "SPECIAL"!

One hour later, we're in the car. I wish I knew where we were going.

PLEASE DON'T BE THE HOSPITAL PLEASE PLEASE PLEASE...

AUDIOLOGY

WHEW! IT'S NOT THE HOSPITAL!

THAT MAN SURE LOOKS LIKE A DOCTOR TO ME!

The man who isn't a doctor but looks like one shows me a big bell...

...and then he puts a blindfold on me.

Then it gets *really* strange. The man puts headphones on my ears...

...and motions for me to go inside a booth.

I don't want to!

But I do.

An amazing thing happens inside the booth: I hear a beep! A real beep! It's the first sound I've heard since the hospital. And then I hear something that sounds sort of like talking, but it's all *weird*.

RAAY YOE HANN WAH OOO EER AAH BEEP!

HUH? *OH!* MAYBE HE SAID "RAISE YOUR HAND WHEN YOU HEAR A BEEP." I'LL TRY THAT...

BEEP

Booop

ooooooP

BEEP!

And then we're done.

The man shows me and my parents a chart he has filled out. My parents don't seem too happy after that.

Then the man squirts some goop into each of my ears...

...and I wait...and I wait and wait...

...until the man pulls the firmed-up goop out of my ears.

And then we're done.

One week later...

AGAIN?

Today the man shows me a little box with cords attached to it.

He puts the little box in an ugly green pouch—and then he puts the little pouch on me.

He puts those funny-looking ear globs—the ones he made last week—back into my ears.

Then he pushes a button...

...and adjusts a dial—

EERS DEE HALOOM UNOLL, JUSS ACK ON AH EEHEE SET—ETT ILLY EEZEE! AH HINK ILL LAHK AYRIN ESS MODEL, ETT ONE UH DEE ESS AID HOUT THAR...

19

CAN. YOU. HEAR. ME?

I UNDERSTOOD THAT! WOW!

YES!

BUT HOW DOES IT LOOK?

ummmm...

Luckily, the man gives me a beautiful pouch for the little box...

...and another lollipop. Gee, I can really hear! But will I *look* good, too?

I CAN HEAR MYSELF EATING THIS LOLLIPOP!

When I get home, I put my bathing suit back on, and I put the little box into the cute pouch.

I strap the whole thing on. I put the ear globs in my ears, and I look in the mirror.

Hmmm. Not great...but not bad, either.

THOSE *CORDS*, THOUGH!

three

I find out that the little box is called a "hearing aid." It's hard to get used to. Everything sounds funny when I use it. Even me!

EEEP.
BOOP. OOP.
EEEP?
HELLO.
HELLO?
AH!
AH!

I don't like the way my hearing aid looks, either, so I cover it up with some "real" clothes. I'm going to visit my friend Emma today. I haven't seen her since I got sick.

BUT HOW AM I GONNA HIDE THE CORDS? *HMMM...*

Emma and I have always looked different from each other, but in ways that didn't matter.

BOY! EMMA SURE IS A LOT TALLER THAN ME IN THIS PICTURE!

Emma & Cece, August 1974

Cece & Emma, February 1975

And *now*? Now we look a *lot* different, and in a way that *does* matter. To me, at least.

I THIG YOO LOO GOO!

HUH?

AH ZEDD, AH THIG YOO LOO GOOOO!

EH SOUNZ LAH YUR UNNAH WAWAH!

HEY! I DIDN'T KNOW YOU'D STILL BE ABLE TO TALK!

YOU SOUND A LITTLE *FUNNY*, THOUGH...

I TALK DIFFERENT, TOO? OH NO.

At the end of summer, it's time to start kindergarten. I now have definite proof that Emma and I are different: she gets on one bus...

...and I get on another.

I don't know where Emma goes, but I take a terrifying bus ride holding the hand of a mysterious woman with a serious afro.

The bus stops in front of what I think is my new school.

The woman from the bus leads me down a hallway.

I JUST *KNOW* EVERYONE IS LOOKING AT ME!

We stop at a door. This must be my new classroom. I'm afraid to look up. But I do.

SHE'S GOT CORDS STICKING OUT OF *HER* EARS, TOO!

HI! I'M WENDY!

And look! *Everyone* here is just like me!

Our teacher is beautiful. We get to call her by her first name.

HELLO! I AM YOUR TEACHER, DORN!

And she looks like *Snow White*! Soon, I adore Dorn every bit as much as the seven dwarfs adored the *real* Snow White. Dorn teaches us math...

...and reading...

...and writing. The basics!

But Dorn also tries to teach us how to lip-read. She says that lip-reading is watching people's mouths move when they talk, so we can understand them better.

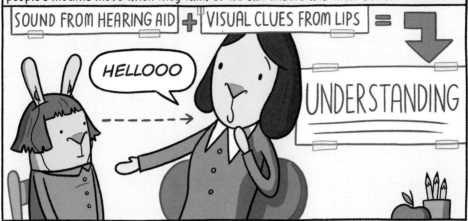

SOUND FROM HEARING AID + VISUAL CLUES FROM LIPS =

HELLOOO

UNDERSTANDING

But this gets tricky, because many words sound similar and people's lips look the same when they are saying them:

MOP, MOB, MOM, BOP, BOB, POP, OR POM?

VASE OR FACE?

SHERRY, CHERRY, OR JERRY?

SUE OR ZOO?

Dorn explains how we're going to figure out what people might be saying.

I SEE A BEAR. I SEE A PEAR. "BEAR" AND "PEAR" LOOK THE SAME COMING OUT OF A PERSON'S MOUTH, DON'T THEY? YOU CAN'T JUST WATCH A PERSON'S LIPS. YOU HAVE TO BE A DETECTIVE AND WATCH FOR OTHER CLUES, TOO.

bear pear

I AM READY!

bear

VISUAL CLUES
What do you see while a person talks to you?

A PEAR.

A BEAR.

CONTEXT CLUES
Where are you while a person talks to you? What's going on around you during the conversation?

A PEAR.

A BEAR.

HELLO!

GESTURAL CLUES
What does a person do with her hands and body while she talks to you? What kinds of faces does she make?

A PEAR.

A BEAR.

HUH?

BUT...

sometimes what a person is *doing* doesn't match up with what it *looks like* they're saying. It's easy to make mistakes!

I SEE A PEAR!!!

MMM! I SEE A BEAR!!!

YUCK!

So Dorn encourages us to practice at home.

BEAR.

care
share

PEAR?

bear
care
share

I make many discoveries about lip-reading:

OOBA LUB JUKKA ___ WA MURMA ARF BR___ PP LO MOOFA U___ M

① MUST SEE PERSON'S FACE AT ALL TIMES!

HUH-AYE. HUH-OW. ARRR. YOOOO?

② EXAGGERATED MOUTH MOVEMENTS ARE CONFUSING!

But wait! There's more!

31

GRRR...

FOO BAH GAH BEE AHFAH!

③ SHOUTING IS **NOT** GOOD!

MUFFA UFFA WUFFA HOW BUH WUH MAH UFFA BUFFA.

④ MUSTACHES AND BEARDS ARE BAD NEWS! (SORRY, DAD.)

HEE HEE GOB HAH GOOBAH BUBBY UBBA LAH MAH BOP!

Leaf Journal

⑤ HANDS IN FRONT OF MOUTH ARE ALSO BAD NEWS!

WUH ARR YOOO BEE LA SHOO MAH WA.

⑥ WHEN IT GETS DARK, GIVE UP!

And finally:

⑦ GROUP DISCUSSIONS ARE IMPOSSIBLE TO UNDERSTAND.

But I can't really make signs like these—I can't even *read* yet! It's hard to explain all this to anybody—except at school.

32

George, Sabrina, Terry, Wendy, Fred, and Jamie: they understand. Because they are just like me.

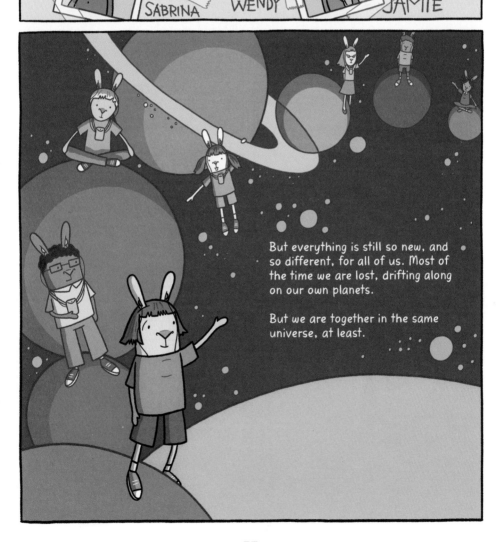

But everything is still so new, and so different, for all of us. Most of the time we are lost, drifting along on our own planets.

But we are together in the same universe, at least.

Suddenly, summer is here again. When I say good-bye to my friends at Fisher School, I do not realize that I will never again be surrounded by kids who are just like me.

The next day, I'm back in the neighborhood with Emma.

ARE YOU READY FOR SUPPER?

SUPPER!? BUT IT'S STILL MORNING!

NO—NOT SUPPER—SUMMER! *SUMMMMMM-MMMMMER!*

SUPPER! HEE HEE!

SIGH.

four

Soon after I say good-bye to my friends at Fisher School, I say good-bye to Emma, too.

BYE, EMMA. BYE, SNOOPY.

My family is moving.

We're leaving our small row house in the big city...

Roanoke

...for a big old house in a small town.

WOW.

My siblings and I meet some of the kids in our new neighborhood.

MAH MOM ADE YAW UM EL-HO!

ATT MAN OR OOPER MAN?

WHAT'RE THOSE *THINGS* COMING OUT OF HER *EARS?*

SHHH!

HMPH. I HEARD WHAT *THAT* ONE SAID JUST FINE.

And I soon discover that these neighborhood kids are *crazy* about their radio!

YAY!

One of the kids tries to be nice and turns up the radio super loud for me.

THERE! HOW'S THAT?

Here's what I *wish* I could say:

THANKS, BUT I CAN *HEAR* THE RADIO WITH MY HEARING AID JUST FINE! I JUST CAN'T *UNDERSTAND* IT, BECAUSE I CAN'T SEE THE FACES OF THE PEOPLE WHO ARE SINGING AND TALKING!

Here's what I *actually* say:

UH...THANKS.

36

So, the neighborhood kids sing along with the songs...

DON'T GO BREAKIN' MAH HEART! I COULDN'T IF I TRIED! OOH, OOH...

...and they laugh along with whoever is talking...

NAW BOPPA MO

HA HA HA HEE HA HEE HA HO

...and it all sounds like a foreign language to me.

MEE NEEBO OP SHHH OP UKKA BIP GOBBA MO GLOP OP GA AW FOOM BUMM OH

HUH?

The person on the radio says something...the kids laugh some more. And this time, so do I. But what about?

HA HA HA HA SO FUNNY HA HA HO HEE HEE HO HO HA

HEH HEH HA AH...

I can't explain it, but it's not just the radio situation that is making me feel so lonely in this new place. It's a feeling that lasts all summer long.

♪ ♪ ♪ HA HA ♪♪ ♪ HA

Summer ends. I find out that I will soon start first grade in a new school.

WILL I BE IN A CLASS LIKE DORN'S CLASS?

NO, SWEETIE. THEY DON'T HAVE A CLASS LIKE THAT IN YOUR NEW SCHOOL. BUT YOU'LL BE GOING TO SCHOOL WITH YOUR NEW NEIGHBORHOOD FRIENDS!

YOU'RE GETTING A BRAND-NEW, SUPER-POWERFUL, JUST-FOR-SCHOOL HEARING AID THAT WILL HELP YOU HEAR BETTER!

IS IT SMALLER THAN THIS ONE?

WELL, IT'S BIGGER, BUT YOU'LL HEAR SO MUCH MORE! AND YOU CAN WEAR THE LITTLE ONE AT HOME!

THE NEIGHBORHOOD KIDS? A BIGGER AID?

Mom walks me to school on the first day. We've been here once before, and I already know where my classroom is. But I'm still scared.

I wear my favorite striped shirt. And underneath that shirt...

HAVE A GREAT DAY!

...well hidden, I hope, is my brand-new, superpowerful, just-for-school hearing aid: The Phonic Ear.

BYE, MAMA.

the Phonic Ear is under here!

X-RAY VIEW this way...

38

The Phonic Ear is paired with a microphone that my teacher, Mrs. Lufton, is supposed to wear. When Mrs. Lufton speaks into the microphone, it sends signals to the Phonic Ear. These signals end up sounding like Mrs. Lufton is talking right in my ear!

HELLO! WELCOME TO THE FIRST GRADE!

MICROPHONE

HELLO! WELCOME TO THE FIRST GRADE!

Mom was right! The Phonic Ear makes Mrs. Lufton's voice louder, just for me. It even *clarifies* her voice—really *sharpens* it! Even when I don't see Mrs. Lufton's face, I understand *every word* she says without having to lip-read at all.

CECE, IS THE MICROPHONE WORKING?

CECE, IS THE MICROPHONE WORKING?

YES!

...I CAN USE MY OWN CRAZY TECHNOLOGY—THE *PHONIC EAR*—TO TURN *MYSELF* INTO A *SUPERHERO*, TOO! MY POWER? *SUPER HEARING!*

44

45

Superheroes might be awesome, but they are also *different*.

And being different feels a lot like being alone.

With the Phonic Ear, I have super hearing. Without it, I can't hear. *Am I deaf?*

five

First grade is really lonely at first.

Wherever I am...

...it feels like I'm always inside my bubble.

Is everyone staring at my hearing aid? At me?

48

49

Best Friends According to Laura is fun.

THAT'S SO NICE!

THANKS!

Sometimes.

MINE'S A BIT *PRETTIER*, THOUGH, DON'TCHA THINK?

UM... OK.

SHE'S CUTE!

THIS IS MISS BUNN!

MISS BUNN? *HA*, THAT'S A WEIRD NAME.

LET'S BUILD A SNOWMAN!

YEAH!

NO, NO! THE CARROT GOES *HERE!* IT'S A *NOSE*, SILLY!

Being best friends with Laura isn't perfect, but it sure beats being in the bubble. We stay best friends all through first grade, and we're still best friends during second grade. One day after school, Laura says:

YOU *HAVE* TO COME TO GIRL SCOUTS WITH ME TODAY. YOU'LL *LOVE* IT!

UM... OK?

I join the Girl Scouts

Girl Scout Service Day

Camping at Dark Hollow

52

The following Saturday, at Laura's house...

BYE, MAMA!

WE'RE HAVING MAC AND CHEESE FOR SUPPER! AND WE'RE GONNA MAKE A CUSHION FORT!

HEY, LET'S PLAY THE DINING ROOM GAME WITH MY SISTER LUCY...

UM... WHAT'S THAT?

WELL, YOU AND LUCY JUST KINDA MARCH AROUND THE TABLE.

IS THAT IT?

IT'LL GET BETTER. *HEE HEE!* JUST KEEP ON MARCHING!

I am glad to be back home after that sleepover!

DID YOU HAVE A GOOD TIME WITH LAURA?

OH?

WELL... NOT REALLY.

RING RING RING

IT'S LAURA. SHE WANTS TO PRETEND TO BE TWINS TOMORROW. SHE SAYS TO WEAR YOUR GREEN GIRL SCOUT T-SHIRT WITH YOUR RED SHORTS WITH THE WHITE STRIPES ON THE SIDE. OH, AND GREEN BARRETTES...

WAH WAH BOOLA BAH WA WAH

OH, SHOOT. THAT DOES SOUND FUN.

The next day...

Monday

IT WORKED! WE'RE TWINS!

SEE? WE'RE JUST LIKE SUSAN AND SHARON IN THE PARENT TRAP!

Tuesday

YEAH! WAIT—WHO?

OK. TOMORROW, WEAR YOUR BLUE SHIRT AND YOUR LEVI'S.

Wednesday

UM, SURE.

THIS IS SO MUCH FUN!

THIS IS STARTING TO GET OLD...

OH! WHERE'S YOUR PALE BLUE SHIRT? YOU WERE SUPPOSED TO WEAR YOUR PALE BLUE SHIRT!

Thursday

YOU JUST SAID BLUE!

55

56

Do I really want to spend any more nights with Laura?

Friends with Laura?	
Yes	No
1. Gave me Fritos in furst grade	1. Vary pushy.
2. Does not care about hearing aid	2. Bad time
3. Good times.	3. More bad times (F...
	4. Twin stuff

It *is* nice that Laura really doesn't seem to notice or care about the hearing aid...

...but a familiar feeling has returned.

WELL?

1. Vary pushy.
2. Bad times
3. More bad times (Fluff...
4. Twin stuff
5. I am Lonely

I THOUGHT BEING BEST FRIENDS WITH LAURA WOULD BE A GOOD THING...

...BUT NOW I'M JUST *SO TIRED* OF BEING *PUSHED AROUND!*

WHAT WOULD BATMAN DO?

IT'S TIME TO *PUSH BACK!*

IT *IS* TIME TO PUSH BACK!

An evil smile crosses our hero's face as she hypnotizes Laura, aka Super Bossypants, with the Phonic Ear's Vicious Feedback Squeal!

With the speed of light, our hero hurls the Earmolds of Virtue at Super Bossypants...

TAKE *THAT*!

...and ties her up with the Cords of Intuition!

BWAH-HAH!

LUCKILY, I HAVE A *SPARE SET* OF *MOLDS AND CORDS* WITH WHICH TO *HEAR* YOUR *FEAR*!

GULP!

UNLEASH THE *HOUND OF HORROR*!

A dazed Super Bossypants shudders in terror when she realizes her fate!

six

The summer after second grade, I get new behind-the-ear hearing aids to use at home. No more little hearing aid in the pouch for me! I'm excited until...

THESE ARE GREAT, MR. RIDENHOUR! CAN I USE 'EM AT SCHOOL?

ER, NO. THESE AREN'T LOUD ENOUGH—OR CLEAR ENOUGH. YOU'LL UNDERSTAND YOUR TEACHER A LOT BETTER WITH THE PHONIC EAR.

RATS. I WAS HOPING TO BE DONE WITH THESE DUMB CORDS AT SCHOOL, TOO.

What I *don't* get that summer is a new friend. Here's what summer with Laura feels like:

HEY! LET'S: A) WALK TO THE 7-ELEVEN! B) GO SWIMMING! C) MAKE MILKSHAKES! D) SING THE DO-RE-MI SONG!

THOSE ALL SOUND FUN! I'LL BITE!

I AM THE WORM OF GOOD TIMES!

GOTCHA!

UH-OH!

OK, NOW WE CAN DO A, B, C, OR D—BUT MY WAY, *RIGHT*?

GLUB.

HOW DO I GET OUT OF THIS?

The night before the first day of third grade, I say a little prayer:

DEAR GOD, I AM READY FOR A NEW FRIEND THIS YEAR. PLEASE, COULD YOU WORK IT SO THAT LAURA AND I ARE IN DIFFERENT CLASSES? THANK YOU, AMEN.

My prayers are answered!

WHO'DJA GET?

MRS. IKLEBERRY.

OH NO! I GOT MRS. BLAIR!

WHEW!

WELL, WE'LL STILL GET TOGETHER AFTER SCHOOL, RIGHT?

UM...YEAH. SURE!

But maybe I should've been more careful with that prayer.

I'VE SPENT SO MUCH TIME WITH LAURA, I DON'T *KNOW* ANYONE ELSE! AND ARE THEY STARING AT MY *CORDS*?

A few weeks after school starts up, a new girl joins our class.

CLASS, THIS IS GINNY. SHE JUST MOVED HERE FROM GEORGIA. SAY HELLO, EVERYONE. GINNY, HAVE A SEAT THERE NEXT TO CECE.

...NEXT TO CECE.

UM...HI.

HI.

It feels like Ginny is always watching me.

In fact, she watches me for weeks...

HERE'S THE MICROPHONE, MRS. IKLEBERRY.

...until finally she asks:

IS. THAT. AAAY. HEAR-ING. AAAID?

OH...UM... I GUESS.

RATS!

62

One day after school, Laura comes over.

I'M GLAD I COULD COME OVER!

YEAH. IT'S BEEN A WHILE...

On our way upstairs, we hear some strange sounds coming from the kitchen.

HEE HEE ha ha hee Snort!

HUH?

WHAT'S THAT?

It's Mom! And some strange woman I've never seen before...

HEE!

HA!

MOM? SMOKING?

GIRLS, THIS IS MRS. WAKELEY! YOU MIGHT KNOW HER DAUGHTER GINNY, FROM SCHOOL?

Ginny? Oh, I know Ginny.

GIRLS, SHOW GINNY UPSTAIRS. MRS. WAKELEY AND I HAVE SOME MORE TALKING TO DO.

HEE HEE!

63

UM, *GINNY*, RIGHT? WELL, CECE AND I HAVE BEEN BEST FRIENDS EVER SINCE FIRST GRADE! AND I'M SPENDING THE NIGHT WITH CECE THIS COMING WEEKEND, *RIGHT, CECE?*

UM...YEAH, I GUESS SO, IF YOU WANT.

OH-KAAAY...

Up in my room, Ginny spots something:

HEY! IS. THAT. A. RICH-ARD. SCA-RRY. BOOK? I. LOVE. RIC-HARD. SCA-RRY!

ME, TOO!

WHY IS SHE TALKING TO ME LIKE THAT? SHE DOESN'T TALK TO *LAURA* THAT WAY!

RICHARD SCARRY!?!? I CAN'T BELIEVE YOU GUYS *LIKE* THOSE BOOKS. THOSE BOOKS ARE FOR BABIES. THEY'RE *BABY BOOKS!*

I WASN'T TALKING TO *YOU*, LAURA.

WOW! DID SHE JUST SAY THAT?

AN-Y-WAAY. I. HAVE. AAY. BU-SY-TOWN. PLAAY-SET. MAY-BE. YOU. CAN. COME. AND. PLAAY. WITH. IT.

65

My mother and Mrs. Wakeley are fast becoming best friends. This means that Ginny and I are spending a lot of time together, too. We discuss important matters...

WAN-NA SEE MEEE MAKE AAARM-PIT FAARTS?

...we play with our stuffed animals...

KISSY, KISSY!

...and we laugh over just about anything.

HA HA! NOW IT SAYS, "GEE, YOUR HAIR *SMELLS!*" HEE HEE!

Ginny even joins my Girl Scout troop.

ALICE THE CAMEL HAS FORTY HUMPS!

YOU *ARE* SPENDING THE NIGHT TONIGHT, *RIGHT?*

UM, GINNY ALREADY ASKED ME TO. SORRY.

I really, really like Ginny. She's funny. She's weird. We love all the same things. So what's the problem? It's the way she talks to me—and the way she talks *about* me.

CEE-CEE. DOO YOO WANT MYYY PEEA-NUT BUTT-ER SAND-WICH?

UM, NO THANKS.

ARGH! I REALLY NEED TO TELL GINNY TO STOP TALKING TO ME LIKE THAT!

CEE-CEE, THIS IS *KREEE*-STEN!

BUT WHAT IF I DO TELL HER AND I HURT HER FEELINGS? I DON'T WANT TO MAKE HER MAD AT ME!

CEE-CEE IS MY DEAF FRIEND. SHE IS ACT-U-A-LLY ONE OF MY BEST-EST FRIENDS!

GULP! GOOD GRIEF! I HAVE TO TELL HER. TOMORROW. MAYBE.

I said I would tell her tomorrow. Well, it's tomorrow. What am I gonna do?

HEY! LET'S LIS-TEN TO MY BRO-THER'S MON-TEEE PY-THON RE-CORD!

OH NO.

HA HA HA! I'LL EX-PLAIN IT IN A SEC!

HEH HEH HEH.

LET MEEE STOP THE RE-CORD NOW...THEY ARE SING-ING AAY SONG THAT GOES, "I'M A LUM-BER-JACK AND I'M OOH-KAY...

♫ ... I SLEEEP ALL NIGHT AAND I WORK AAALL DAAAY!" HAR!

THIS IS TOTALLY DRIVING ME *NUTS!*

HI-LAR-I-OUS, RIGHT?

HEH, YEAH.

AND NOW FOR THE NEXT BIT!

OH? UM...YAY?

RATS.

Panel 1: I'm so frustrated with Ginny!

SNORT!

Panel 2: She can hear and understand everything so easily.

I LOVE THIS PART!

HA HA!

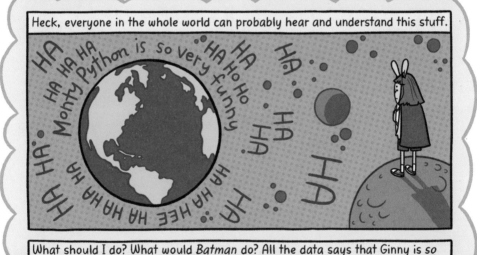

Heck, everyone in the whole world can probably hear and understand this stuff.

Monty Python is so very funny

HA HA HA HA HA HA HA HA HA HA HEE HA HA HA HO HO HA HA HA

What should I do? What would *Batman* do? All the data says that Ginny is *so close* to being a perfect friend. But obviously, there *is* a problem:

GOOD:	NOT SO GOOD:
SO FUNNY	MAKES A *HUGE* DEAL ABOUT MY HEARING!
WEIRD IN A GOOD WAY	
LIKES THE THINGS I LIKE	*AAAAHHH!!!*

71

School. Friends. *No friends.* The Phonic Ear. It's all so *exhausting.* I need a break.

So I watch TV.

I watch anything that's on. *Everything*, in fact. Soap operas. Cartoons. Old sitcoms. New sitcoms. Dramas. Even commercials! And the crazy thing is...

...I love TV...

...even though it's so hard to understand what the people on it are saying!

HUH?

TV isn't like the weird foreign movies that Dad takes me to every once in a while.

ENGLISH SUBTITLES!!

OOOH! *WORDS!* I *LOVE* THEM!

URM...I'M NOT SURE THESE MOVIES ARE ALL THAT *APPROPRIATE* FOR YOU... THAT WAS A *LOT* OF SKIN...

BUT, DAD, I *LOVE* HAVING THE WORDS! I ACTUALLY KNOW WHAT'S GOING ON!

Sadly, TV does *not* have subtitles.

HUH?

UGGA MAWHAW OOP AH GAH MUMMA MUH GOO AH OH MEEMO...

I *try* to lip-read the people on TV...

C'MON! JUST ONE WORD?

BAB! MUMMA MAW! GOOBA BOO AH

...but it's really, *really* hard to do!

WHAT IN *HECK* IS GOING ON?

73

I keep watching, though. Some shows are fairly easy to lip-read, like soap operas:

Actor's face takes up the whole screen: easy to see lips!

Actor speaks slowly and dramatically...

...and it's pretty much a guarantee that LOVE will come up!

But who wants to watch *soap operas*? They're so mushy...

BUT...I *NEED* YOU, JIM!

AND I WANT TO HAVE...

...A *BABY* WITH YOU!

UM, SORRY. I LOVE *WANDA!*

...and so boring!

IT'S THIRTY MINUTES LATER...

...AND WE'RE STILL HAVING THE SAME CONVERSATION!

I OBVIOUSLY NEED TO FIND SOMETHING BETTER TO WATCH!

Aha! Cartoons! I *love* cartoons! But *lip-reading* cartoons? Impossible!

BLAH WAH FRED LOO MA WAH HA HOOH WALAWA...

Cartoon lips are not like real lips at *all*. Not even close.

OOGA MOO BLAH HAH GOO BOO HAW!

Unreadable!

But I love cartoons anyway. The characters do so many funny things that I can *see*.

And hey, check it out! Here's a cartoon that doesn't have any talking at all!

Cat doesn't talk!

Mouse doesn't talk, either!

But as much as I love cartoons, even they can be pretty boring sometimes.

IT'S SAFE TO SAY THAT THE CAT REALLY, *REALLY* WANTS TO CATCH THE MOUSE. AGAIN.

I watch other shows on TV, too, even if they are not as easy to understand as soap operas and cartoons. I might catch a few of the words in these shows, but not many.

I see the person's face while she's talking. She looks worried. But she's talking so fast, and her lips are so small on the TV screen, that I can't understand her. Is John-Boy lost—or something worse?

MA! WE OOK EBBER WAR AN WE ANT FINE JOHN-BOY!

Uh-oh! Now I can see a different person's face. She is listening to someone who is talking—and that person is OFFSCREEN! Will John-Boy be OK?

UGGA SHUFFA GOO BLAH BLAH HA OOKIN WAMAH WAH!

Now I can mostly just see the speaker's REAR END!

AGGA BOOP BAH WAHAH BICK! CHUBBA UBB OH GOBBA!

WHO KNOWS WHAT'S GOING ON NOW? I SURE CAN'T LIP-READ A BUTT!

Now NOBODY on the TV is talking. But I think I hear something that sounds like talking! It's the... dreaded VOICE-OVER!

AN GOO HON BOY GABBA WAH GAH WHA BEE GOO BA BA MAMA.

I STILL HAVE NO IDEA WHAT HAPPENED TO JOHN-BOY!

If I'm watching TV with somebody who doesn't know me well, like a neighborhood kid whose mom is visiting my mom, then that kid almost always asks:

YOU'RE THE KID WHO CAN'T HEAR, RIGHT? WHY NOT JUST TURN UP THE VOLUME?

OH BROTHER. HOW CAN I EXPLAIN THIS?

Well, here's what happens when I turn up the TV:

WAH BESS MAH WAWA GAH ANDY! YOO GOOLA FA BERRY GAH BOOLA!

Before

WAH BESS MAH WAWA GAH ANDY! YOO GOOLA FA BERRY GAH BOOLA!

Same scene, with volume UP!

UM, IT DOESN'T MATTER HOW *LOUD* IT IS. IT'S JUST HARD TO UNDERSTAND, I GUESS.

SO WHY ARE YOU WATCHING IT, THEN?

um...

Well, I guess I watch TV because the folks on it are there for me whenever I want them—and they don't care if I can hear them or not!

OINK!

Not so there for me are my older siblings—Ashley and Sarah. They are often busy doing mysterious older-kid things:

WANNA PLAY OLD MAID?

HUH? UH...NOT REALLY.

DO YOU WANNA PLAY OLD MAID?

UH...NO!

AND DON'T YOU *DARE* TELL MOM!

But when they *aren't* busy, they watch TV. A *lot* of TV. If I want to spend any time with Ashley and Sarah, it's gotta be while watching TV. So that's what I do.

79

However, the shows that Ashley and Sarah watch are impossible to understand.

MURK PROOP TIBBA MAWHAW...

SHMAR MUMBAMUMBA GUMBA...

But luckily they are nice enough to tell me what the people on TV are saying...

...without ever being obnoxious about it.

Every now and then, ABC shows an hour-long movie made especially for kids.

Sometimes these movies are super corny. We *really* love the ones that are.

HAR! THIS ONE'S GONNA BE *GOOD*!

When this one starts—*wait a minute!* Is she wearing what I *think* she's wearing?

I CAN'T BELIEVE IT! SOMEONE LIKE *ME*— ON THE *TV*!

YOO AH AH EFFO! MUMMBA GUH!

WHAT JUST HAPPENED? WHAT DID SHE *SAY*?

I GOTTA GO PEE... HIC! HEE HEE...

WHEW! DEAFO, HUH?

HEH HEH...WELL, IF THAT KID IS "DEAFO"...

...AM I "DEAFO" TOO?

84

A few weeks after my argument with Ginny, I see her handing out little cards. I wonder what they say. Will I get one, too?

UH—SORRY A-BOUT EAR-LI-ER. HERE.

SHE'S STILL TALKING FUNNY? OH WELL.

You're invited!

What. birthday party sleepover

When. Friday. April 6

Where. Ginny's.

A BIRTHDAY PARTY AND A SLEEPOVER? WOWEE!

UH...

A SLEEPOVER, HUH?

After a long week of waiting, the day of the sleepover is finally here! I pack as soon as I get home from school.

OH BOY!

Packing List:

toothpaste (possibly just for show)
toothbrush

cute pj's

clean shirt for tomorrow

Pill-pill

sleeping bag

extra hearing aid batteries (I do NOT want to run down and miss everything!!!)

clean underwear

Socks

Miss Bunn (may need to keep hidden??)

birthday present for Ginny!

...UM, I GOTTA GO...YES, YES—LISTEN, CECE IS *BREATHING* ON ME— OK—BYE!

OK ALREADY! WE'RE GOING!

HAVE FUN! AND JUST ASK MRS. WAKELEY TO CALL ME IF YOU NEED ANYTHING.

I'LL BE FINE, MOM!

BYE!

HI!

SO, WHO ALL'S HERE?

YOU'RE THE FIRST, AC-TU-A-LLY. BUT IT'LL BE CAR-RIE, ELL-EN, AND MISS-Y. I CAN'T *BE-LIEVE* MISS-Y'S COM-ING—SHE IS SO POP-U-LAR!

The other guests arrive...

CARRIE

1. Shy, but nice.

2. Draws really good horses.

3. Soft voice. So hard to hear!

UH, HI? I BROUGHT SOME CANDY. WANT SOME?

HUH?

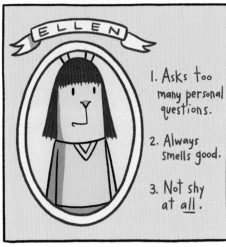

ELLEN

1. Asks too many personal questions.

2. Always smells good.

3. Not shy at all.

WHERE ARE THOSE CORDS THAT ARE USUALLY COMING OUT OF YOUR EARS?

WHY DO YOU WEAR OVERALLS SO MUCH?

ARE YOU *DEATH?*

And then there is...

MISSY

OH! IT'S THE LITTLE *DEAF GIRL* FROM MRS. IKLEBERRY'S CLASS! GINNY'S TOLD ME *ALL ABOUT YOU!*

1. Help.

89

In spite of that rough beginning, I start having a great time at Ginny's sleepover. We celebrate Ginny's birthday...

...and explore her older brother's bedroom...

...and play lots of Twister.

RIGHT HAND *BLOOOOO*, CEE-CEE!

GOOD GRIEF!

But then things start to go downhill again.

HEY! THE *TV GUIDE* SAYS THAT *SOMEWHERE IN TIME* IS COMING ON IN TEN MINUTES! IT'S MY FAVORITE!

OH NO. DID SHE SAY *SOMEWHERE IN TIME*?

SQUEEEEE!

OH! I *LOVE* THAT MOVIE!

UH-OH.

YAY!

EEK!

OH, SO DREAMY!

Oogah blah mumba

ICK.

OH, YOU *POOR THING!* CAN YOU EVEN *HEAR* THE TV?

UH, I CAN *HEAR* IT. I JUST CAN'T UNDERST—

WE'LL JUST *TURN UP THE VOLUME!*

I *CAN* HEAR IT! I JUST CAN'T *UNDERSTAND* IT! AND I'M *NOT* A "POOR THING"!

Thankfully, after all that awfulness, the party starts to get fun again.

...AND YOU SHOULDA SEEN MARY KISSING THAT BOY FROM MS. HUFFMAN'S CLASS! ALL THIS MWAH MWAH MWAH!

HEE HEE!

THIS COULD GET INTERESTING!

SQUEAL!

But then— **CLIK!** —Ginny turns the lights out!

HA HA HEE HEE SQUEE HEE HA HA HO HA HEE HEE!

OH NO!

I CAN TELL THEY'RE LAUGHING, BUT WHAT ABOUT? I NEED TO *SEE!* DID GINNY DO THIS ON PURPOSE? IS SHE *MAD AT ME?*

WELL, *RATS!* IF I ASK GINNY TO TURN THE LIGHTS BACK ON, SHE'LL BE EVEN MADDER AT ME. *EVERYONE* WILL BE MAD AT ME!

HA HA HEE CEE HA HA CEE HA MUMMBA HA HEE CEE HA HA GOBBA WOBBA HA HO HO HEE HA HA!

I *HATE* THIS! ARE THEY TALKING ABOUT *ME*? ARE THEY *LAUGHING* AT ME?

I CAN'T TAKE IT ANYMORE!

I gather up my stuff in the dark, and I feel my way out of the basement...

...and up the stairs.

MRS. WAKELEY? WILL YOU CALL MY MOM? I DON'T FEEL SO GOOD...

I am relieved that Mom doesn't ask any questions on the way home.

UM...HI, DAD. CAN I WATCH TV WITH YOU AND MOM?

Oh, I'm so glad to be home. What a night. I wish I'd told those girls what I think!

Our hero, the mighty *El Deafo*, is tied up by a band of pajama-wearing Super Villains!

The Super Villains interrogate El Deafo—and torture her with more *Somewhere in Time!* But El Deafo is strong...

WHAT ARE THOSE CORDS FOR?

WHY DO YOU WEAR OVERALLS SO MUCH?

ARE YOU **DEATH**?

wah Wah Wah

YES, I'M *DEATH!* AND *YOU* ARE NEXT ON MY LIST!

HERE'S A TASTE OF YOUR OWN ROPE—AND SOME OF THAT *FUNERAL MUSIC* YOU WANTED, TOO!

But it's not over yet for El Deafo! She is accosted by another menacing foe...

EEK!

I AM **SUPERMISSY!** PREPARE FOR BEAUTY, MY LITTLE **DEAF FRIEND!**

Our hero is more than ready!

READ MY LIPS! **NOBODY** TOUCHES THIS FACE!

HOW ABOUT A **MAKEOVER,** MISSY? WHAT PLEASURE THIS GIVES ME, **YOU'LL** NEVER KNOW!

TA-DA!

EEK! I'M HIDEOUS!

At long last, El Deafo faces the mightiest foe of all, the dastardly SuperGinny.

DON'T *EVER* CALL ME YOUR *DEAF FRIEND* AGAIN. OR YOUR *FRIEND*. DID YOU TURN THOSE LIGHTS OFF ON PURPOSE?

I DUNNO.

UH...I'M *SORRY!*

SORRY ISN'T GOOD ENOUGH. GOOD-BYE.

ZZZZZZZZZZZ...

nine

Ah, summer. Three months of freedom. Three months of bliss. Three months of *not* wearing the Phonic Ear.

But summer ends—as it always does—with the beginning of a new year of school.

YAWN

UGH. TIME TO WEAR *THIS* AGAIN!

SIGH...

FOURTH GRADE! I CAN'T BELIEVE IT! ARE YOU EXCITED?

UM, MAYBE A LITTLE...

Actually, except for the Phonic Ear, I am *very* excited. A new year!

BUS

Just like in previous years, our mornings start in the gym. I see Ginny, but I avoid her. I want to sit with kids who don't know me. Maybe I can pass myself off as a hearing person.

But I'm not very good at doing this.

HI, I'M BONNIE. WHAT'S YOUR NAME?

UH—CECE.

WELL, HEY. I'VE TOLD EVERYONE ELSE, SO I MIGHT AS WELL TELL YOU: MY GRANDMA MAKES PIE.

UH...COOL!

WHAT!?

UH...

I SAID, MY GRANDMA MAY DIE!

OH! OH! I AM SO, SO SORRY!

THAT'S OK. SAY! *WAIT A MINUTE—*

I CAN'T BELIEVE I *DID* THAT! ARGH!

—ARE YOU DEAF? IS THAT WHAT THE CORDS ARE FOR?

OH NO!

BECAUSE I...

KNOW...

SIGN LANGUAGE!

HELP.

What's wrong with sign language? *Nothing.* But some of the people doing sign language? At *me? Some* people put on a real *show* when they start signing—almost like *mimes!*

CE—

—CE...

IS ANYONE WATCHING THIS?

...and *some* people end up saying phony-baloney stuff when they sign...

...YOU...

...ARE **SPECIAL!**

PLEASE. STOP.

...and sure enough, when somebody signs at you like that, everybody else *stares* at you!

Argh! I wish I could turn into El Deafo in these situations.

I DO NOT KNOW THESE MYSTERIOUS HAND SIGNALS, STRANGER! BUT I *DO* HAVE A GREAT POWER! I CAN *READ YOUR LIPS!*

GULP!

If only it were that simple.

SOME LIP-READER I AM. *"MAKES PIE"?* GOOD GRIEF.

SNIFF!

Back at home, after a long first day of school...

WELL, HI! HOW WAS SCHOOL?

IT WAS OK. BUT SOME *GIRL* STARTED *SIGNING* AT ME!

OH, CECE. I KNOW YOU DON'T LIKE IT WHEN PEOPLE DO THAT. SHE WAS PROBABLY JUST EXCITED TO MEET SOMEONE LIKE YOU, AND TO SHARE WHAT SHE KNOWS WITH YOU...

SOMEONE LIKE *ME*?

MAYBE *YOU* SHOULD LEARN SIGN LANGUAGE! IT WOULD GIVE YOU A *NEW WAY* TO TALK TO PEOPLE. IT COULD BE *FUN*!

MOM! I DON'T WANT TO!

I HEARD THERE'S A SIGN LANGUAGE CLASS THAT JUST STARTED UP AT CHURCH!

OH *NO*!

MAMA, *PLEASE* DON'T MAKE ME DO THAT!

LET ME LOOK INTO IT FIRST, SWEETIE. IT MIGHT REALLY BE USEFUL TO YOU.

MOM! NO!

106

One evening a few weeks later, Mom takes me to a classroom at our church.

We meet our sign language teacher, Mrs. Blankenship, who, I admit, is very nice.

HELLO!

AND WELCOME—

TO SIGN LANGUAGE!

FIRST, IS ANYONE HERE DEAF OR HARD OF HEARING?

UM—MY DAUGHTER IS...

MOM!

WELL, THAT'S LOVELY. FIRST, LET'S TALK ABOUT AMERICAN SIGN LANGUAGE. IT'S THE MAIN LANGUAGE USED BY DEAF PEOPLE—AND IT IS *VITAL* FOR THEIR COMMUNICATION WITH OTHER DEAF PEOPLE AND WITH THEIR FAMILIES AND FRIENDS.

MANY HEARING FOLKS THINK THAT SIGN LANGUAGE IS A SIMPLE LANGUAGE—BUT THAT IS NOT TRUE AT ALL!

BLAH, BLAH, BLAH—UH-OH!

SIGN LANGUAGE IS QUITE DIFFERENT FROM SPOKEN ENGLISH. IT'S A VERY RICH LANGUAGE—A VERY *COMPLEX* LANGUAGE.

MY HEARING-AID BATTERIES ARE RUNNING DOWN!

WHY DON'T I EVER REMEMBER TO BRING EXTRA BATTERIES?

SO, WE'LL BE LEARNING THE BASICS OF THIS VERY COMPLEX LANGUAGE.

WHEW. LIP-READING IS *HARD* WITHOUT SOUND.

LET'S START WITH THE ALPHABET. HERE'S "A".

HEY, I KNOW *THAT!* THAT'S "A"! I GUESS SHE'S TEACHING THE ALPHABET. *HMPH.*

Thirty long—and silent—minutes later, the class finally ends. I lip-read my mother saying, "What did you think?" I say, "How do I know? My hearing-aid batteries ran down."

And then Mom says, "*See?* Maybe sign language could be useful to you after all!"

↑ ME saying "I don't think so!"

Every Thursday night, I find myself back in that dumb old classroom...

HERE IS "THANK YOU..."

WEEK 2
MANNERS

CE-CE, THANK YOU FOR BE-ING MY FRIEND!

UM... YEAH.

HERE'S A FUN ONE: *GIRAFFE!*

WEEK 3
ANIMALS

THESE ANIMAL SIGNS ARE SO CUTE! TRY ONE!

HMPH.

"elephant"

OK! LET'S PARTNER UP AND ASK EACH OTHER HOW SHE FEELS...

WEEK 4
FEELINGS

HOW AM I *FEELING?* TAKE A WILD GUESS.

"How are you feeling?"

I can't believe that my *own* mother can't see that I am absolutely miserable.

JUST TRY IT—"FATHER"!

WEEK 5 FAMILY

PLEASE?

COME ON, CECE! YOU CAN DO IT!
FATHER!

IT'S REAL EASY, SEE?
FATHER!

ARGH!

GOODNESS, CECE! EVERYONE'S JUST HOPING THAT YOU'LL PARTICIPATE MORE. NEXT WEEK, PLEASE JOIN US. YOU'LL SEE HOW FUN IT IS, OK?

HOW WILL I EVER GET OUT OF THIS?

So what, I haven't been "participating." Mom totally makes up for it—she *loves* to sign!

Enraged, El Deafo busts out of the handcuffs...

...and unfurls her torpedo-like wrath onto her own mother!

KA POW

OW!

OK, OK, YOU'VE MADE YOUR POINT. WE'RE GOING HOME.

DID I REALLY DO THAT?

JESUS IS LOVE

WHAT IN THE *WORLD* WAS *THAT* ALL ABOUT?

OH, MOM— I'M SORRY...

...BUT I *HATE* THAT CLASS! EVERYBODY *SIGNING* AT ME! LIKE I ALREADY KNOW SIGN LANGUAGE, JUST BECAUSE I'M *DEAF!*

NO ONE'S SIGNING *AT* YOU— THEY'RE TRYING TO SIGN *WITH* YOU—TO *HELP* YOU!

WELL, I *HATE* IT!

AND AS FAR AS *"HELPING"*— IT'LL *HELP* PEOPLE *STARE* AT ME, IS WHAT IT'LL DO! "LOOK AT THAT DEAF GIRL! ISN'T SHE *SPECIAL!"*

WELL—YOU *ARE* SPECIAL—

MOM!

—JUST LIKE *EVERY* KID IS SPECIAL.

OH, GOOD GRIEF.

MOM THINKS "SPECIAL" MEANS "GREAT," OR "COOL." IF ONLY! "SPECIAL" MEANS "YOU'RE NOT LIKE ME! YOU'RE *WEIRD!"* I *HATE* THAT WORD!

LISTEN. WE DON'T HAVE TO CONTINUE THE CLASS. JUST DON'T BE SO HARD ON THE PEOPLE WHO TRY TO HELP YOU. SOMEDAY YOU MIGHT ACTUALLY *WANT* THEIR HELP.

WHEW!

We stop for a treat on the way home...

...and then—believe it or not—we see a couple arguing...

...in *sign language!*

THAT IS *AMAZING.*

ten

As I ride the bus home from school one day, I realize just how many kids live on my street. We practically fill up the whole bus! But not one of them is in my grade.

There had been a girl in my class, and we watched *The Monkees* at her house after school sometimes. But she moved away.

The other kids on the street *are* nice, though, especially the older ones. They often include me in their games and stuff...

HEY, WE'RE PLAYING KICKBALL WHEN WE GET HOME. WANNA PLAY?

But *I* think they've been *told* to be nice to the deaf kid. And anyway, I always seem to ruin those games of theirs!

KAH MON!

OH DA *BAW!*

GA WOO! OH ETT!

UH, THANKS. BUT I HAVE A LOT OF HOMEWORK...

OH. OK.

Kickball? *Ha!* I'm gonna do what I usually do after school: watch TV.

CECE, IT'S GINNY. SHE WANTS TO KNOW IF YOU'D LIKE TO COME OVER.

UH—NO THANKS. TELL HER I'M BUSY.

GINNY?—UH—CECE IS KIND OF BUSY TODAY—UH—TELL YOUR MOM HI FOR ME, OK?—BYE...

YOU HAVEN'T SEEN GINNY IN AGES! WHAT'S GOING ON? DID YOU HAVE A FIGHT?

KINDA.

WANT TO TALK ABOUT IT?

NOT REALLY.

WELL, I'M SORRY ABOUT THAT. BUT I DON'T APPRECIATE LYING TO YOUR FRIEND. SO I SUGGEST YOU HURRY UP AND GET *"BUSY."*

I'm relieved that I don't have to get together with Ginny. I guess I *could* play some kickball with the kids down the street. Or not. I don't know *what* to do.

SIGH...

Somehow, being alone is always easier for me. But it's still, well, *lonely!*

OH, WOE...

WHAT I *NEED* IS A SIDEKICK!

THERE'S THAT THIRD-GRADER, MARTHA. I WONDER WHY *SHE'S* NOT PLAYING WITH THE OTHERS? SHE USUALLY DOES...

HEY!

POP

UMM OBA HEE UN TAY ALOO!

UM—HOLD ON A MINUTE!

I *THINK* SHE WANTS ME TO COME OVER...

THIS HERE DIRT SOUP MAKES ME THINK OF *LITTLE HOUSE ON THE PRAIRIE.* DO YOU WATCH THAT SHOW?

I *LOVE* THAT SHOW!

HEY! LET'S PRETEND THAT *WE'RE LITTLE HOUSE ON THE PRAIRIE!* DO YOU WANNA BE MARY OR LAURA?

CAN I BE LAURA?

YEAH! I'LL BE MARY. *WHOA!* THAT SCARLET FEVER DID A *NUMBER* ON ME! JOHN-BOY, THAT YOU?

HA HA HA! JOHN-BOY— HEE HEE! MARTHA, I MEAN *MARY*—YOU'RE IN THE *WRONG SHOW!*

WHAT IF MARY ENDED UP ON *STAR TREK* OR SOMETHING?

BEAM ME BACK TO THE PRAIRIE, SCOTTY!

hee hee ha ha hee hee ha ha

YOU KNOW, IT'S FRIDAY AND ALL— YOU SHOULD ASK YOUR MOM IF YOU CAN SPEND THE NIGHT!

I WAS THINKING THE *EXACT SAME THING!*

122

Yay! Mom said yes to the sleepover! I start packing—and I start thinking, too.

MARTHA IS SO FUNNY! I'M ACTUALLY GLAD SHE'S NOT IN MY GRADE, BECAUSE IF SHE WAS, SHE'D SEE MY GIANT HEARING-AID AND THOSE CORDS COMING OUT OF MY EARS. SHE'D *KNOW* I WAS DEAF. BUT SHE *DOESN'T* KNOW, BECAUSE SHE HASN'T NOTICED MY BEHIND-THE-EAR AIDS. WELL, I *THINK* SHE HASN'T NOTICED. I MEAN, SHE DOESN'T SHOUT AT ME, OR MOVE HER MOUTH ALL FUNNY, OR TRY TO SIGN AT ME. SHE'S NOT BOSSY, EITHER! NO *WAY* AM I GONNA LET HER FIND OUT. IT MIGHT RUIN *EVERYTHING!* OH, WE'RE GONNA HAVE SO MUCH FUN TONIGHT!

YAY!

WE ARE GONNA HAVE SO MUCH FUN TONIGHT!

I WAS JUST THINKING THE *EXACT SAME THING!*

Inside Martha's house...

MOM, THIS IS CECE!

FANCY MEETING *YOU* HERE!

THAT'S MY DAD...

REALLY?

DREAMY!

AND HERE ARE MY LOONY SISTERS! PROTECT ME!

MOM!

DAD'S PICKING UP LONG JOHN SILVER'S AND WE'RE EATING IN FRONT OF THE TV!

A TV SUPPER? *REALLY!?*

YEAH! WHAT WOULD YOU LIKE DAD TO ORDER FOR YOU? A MUMBLE ABBO OR AH ISH UPPA?

HUH? I BETTER PRETEND THAT I KNOW WHAT SHE SAID!

UH...

...I'LL HAVE WHAT YOU'RE HAVING?

OK! TWO FISH SUPPERS COMING RIGHT UP!

FISH? ICK. WELL, AT LEAST MARTHA DOESN'T SUSPECT ANYTHING DIFFERENT ABOUT ME...

124

AHEM! GIRLS, IT IS *WAY* PAST YOUR BEDTIME...

AWWW...

WELL, WE CAN STAY UP AND TALK!

CAN WE LEAVE A LIGHT ON?

SURE THING!

LOOK DOWN YOUR SHIRT AND SPELL "ATTIC"!

A-T-T-I-C? MARTHA *ANN!*

...YOU KNOW WHAT WE SHOULD DO TOMORROW? WE SHOULD WALK DOWNTOWN AND GET CANDY BARS AND DRINKS AND STUFF...AND THEN WE CAN MAKE MORE DIRT SOUP...

...SO SLEEPY...

...AND SO I SAID, WHAT IS THAT AWF STINKIN' SMELL? AND SHE SAYS, WE THAT'LL BE YO SAID THAT! SO EYED LOOK OFF! I FELT

I GOTTA GET SOME SLEEP! SURELY SHE WON'T NOTICE IF I TURN OFF MY AIDS...

CLIK!

AH, SWEET SILENCE...

ZZZZZZZ...

tap tap

UH-OH...

I lip-read Martha saying, "Did you just turn your hearing-aids off on me?"

OH NO! I'VE RUINED EVERYTHING!

ummm... I'M SO SORRY!

CLIK!

WAIT! MARTHA KNOWS ABOUT MY HEARING-AIDS?

eleven

Fourth grade ends, and it's summer! Summertime with Martha is awesome.

WE CAN GET LIMEADES AT THE DRUGSTORE!

OW! UM, YEAH!

Walking downtown in bare feet!

AAAH...

Cooling feet on drugstore floor!

It can't get much better than this!

CHECK OUT MY BEE-HIND!

OOH, FUNKY!

Roller-skating on the sidewalks!

Or can it?

LOOKS LIKE A NEW FAMILY IS MOVING INTO THE CARTERS' OLD HOUSE!

LET'S CHECK IT OUT!

YEAH!

We cross the street. Some other kids have come out to meet the new neighbors, too.

HOLY COW! THEY ARE SO GOOD-LOOKING!

HI!

The new kids look like rock stars! Like the Partridge Family or something!

Or maybe even *movie* stars! Good *grief*, the beauty!

HI! WE'RE THE MILLERS!

Kathy   Caryn   Steve   Mike

I'M MIKE. WHAT'S YOUR NAME?

UH...UH...

THIS IS CECE! SHE LIVES TWO DOORS UP! I'M MARTHA, AND I—

—UH...WE GOTTA GO! COME ON, MARTHA!

HUH?

HEY! I WAS STILL TALKING! WHAT'S THE MATTER? WAIT! OH MY GOSH—YOU LIKE HIM?

WHAT!? NO! NO WAY!

CECE AND THE NEW KID SITTIN' IN A TREE, K-I-S-S-I-N—

MARTHA, STOP!

I DON'T EVEN KNOW THE KID! SO DON'T YOU DARE TELL ANYBODY ANYTHING! 'SPECIALLY NOT MY MOM! 'CAUSE YOU'RE WRONG!

OOH! A WIDDLE BOYFRIEND!

Martha is sorta right. But I'm not going to tell her—or anyone else—that I like this *Mike Miller* very much.

Instead, I decide to spy on him. I want to learn *everything* about him—but *secretly*!

SHHHH!

TOP SECRET FILES

DO NOT OPEN This means You!

I watch Mike Miller very carefully. Day...

EY! ETT ETT UMM ANNY AHH DAH EEEN AHKAH!

UH-HUH...

...after day...

UM...AH OOH OH ENN AAH ERRAH HAH UMBAY EY AAY?

UH-HUH...

...after day!

ETT ER URN A MIR AH OOP!

UH-HUH...

UH...I GOTTA GO. I WANNA WRITE SOMETHING DOWN...

UH-HUH.

This could be it! A real opportunity to talk to *Mike Miller!*

WELL, LET'S GO RIGHT NOW AND ASK HIM IF WE CAN USE THE TRAMPOLINE!

UH... OKAY!

GO ON— KNOCK!

KNOCK KNOCK

HELLO?

UH...

CAN WE JUMP ON THE TRAMPOLINE?

UH...JUMP...

SURE!

LET'S GO! HE SAID YES!

...JUMP...

140

twelve

It is a very bouncy summer. Sometimes I jump on the trampoline by myself...

...but most of the time, I jump with Martha.

WE SHOULD ASK MIKE TO JUMP WITH US SOMETIME!

NOW, WHY WOULD WE DO *THAT*?

BECAUSE YOU *LIKE* HIM?

NOT *THAT* MUCH! HEE HEE!

I quickly change the subject...

WHEW! LET'S DO SOMETHING ELSE!

HOW ABOUT TAG? BETCHA CAN'T CATCH ME!

YOU'RE **ON!**

HEE HEE!

HEY! NO FAIR! I'M STILL STUCK ON THE TRAMP!

WHOOP!

I'VE ALMOST GOT HER NOW!

OW!

I come back from the doctor's office with eye medicine and a fancy eye patch.

CAN I GO SHOW MARTHA MY NEW EYE PATCH? SHE'LL LOVE IT!

GREAT IDEA!

HEE HEE! SHE'LL LAUGH WHEN SHE SEES *THIS*!

KNOCK KNOCK

Martha answers the door.

AHOY THERE, MATEY! I LOOK LIKE A PIRATE, DON'TCHA THINK?

UH... UH...

145

DID SHE JUST *THROW UP*? IT DOESN'T LOOK *THAT* BAD, DOES IT?

And then—Martha disappears!

MARTHA? ANYBODY?

I wait a bit, and then Martha's mom comes.

I'M SO SORRY ABOUT YOUR EYE! LISTEN, MARTHA ISN'T REALLY UP TO TALKING JUST YET. SHE KIND OF THINKS THAT ALL OF THIS IS HER FAULT!

OH, BUT IT *ISN'T* HER FAULT! NOT AT *ALL*! IT WAS AN *ACCIDENT*!!

I CAME OVER TO SHOW HER THAT I'M *FINE*! HONEST!

I KNOW, HONEY, I KNOW. DON'T WORRY. SHE'LL COME AROUND.

SNIFF!

146

The next day, I write Martha a note. I put a koala bear sticker on it, too. She'll like that!

Dear Martha,

How are you? I am fine, and so is my eye. It was NOT your fault!!!!

At all!!!

I miss you.

Love, Cece

I run across the street to give her the note. I don't even wait for Mom to watch me.

MARTHA— **WAIT!**

HI, CECE. UM...MARTHA IS STILL UPSET. BUT SHE'LL COME AROUND. IS THAT NOTE FOR HER?

PLEASE WILL YOU GIVE IT TO HER?

OF COURSE, DEAR.

The next day...

HEARD ANYTHING FROM MARTHA?

NO. WILL YOU TRY CALLING HER FOR ME?

...UM, YES, PATSY, I SEE. WELL, TELL HER THAT CECE REALLY, REALLY MISSES HER AND THAT SHE DOESN'T BLAME MARTHA ONE BIT... OK, SURE. BYE.

I'M SO SORRY...

SHE'LL **NEVER** "COME AROUND."

147

I try to give Martha some time, but one week later, I'm back at her door.

MY EYE'S ALL BETTER! SURELY WHEN SHE SEES THAT, SHE'LL BE MY FRIEND AGAIN!

KNOCK KNOCK KNOCK

MARTHA? LOOK! I'M ALL BETTER! NO MORE EYE PATCH!

UH, I GOTTA GO. I THINK MY MOM'S CALLING ME...

MARTHA, *COME BACK HERE!* ARE YOU GONNA BE LIKE THIS FOR THE REST OF THE SUMMER?

OR FOREVER?

I'M QUITTING THE SIDEKICK BUSINESS...

QUITTING!? YOU CAN'T *DO* THAT! YOU *PINKIE SWORE!* WHAT ABOUT THE *PINKIE SWEAR??*

I UNDID MY PINKIE SWEAR WHEN I HURT YOUR EYE, EL DEAFO! AND I JUST CAN'T DEAL WITH THE *GUILT!*

BUT YOU *DIDN'T* HURT MY EYE! AND IT'S ALL BETTER! IT'S *NOBODY'S FAULT!*

THEN *I'M* NOBODY. GOOD-BYE, EL DEAFO!

OH *NO!*

WHAT AM I GONNA DO WITHOUT HER?

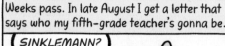

thirteen

Weeks pass. In late August I get a letter that says who my fifth-grade teacher's gonna be.

SINKLEMANN? HUH. GEE WHIZ, SUMMER IS GONNA BE OVER SOON...

...AND STILL NOT EVEN A *PEEP* FROM MARTHA.

RING RING

BUT WAIT! COULD IT BE?

WELL, YES! SHE'D *LOVE* THAT. YES—YES, IT *HAS* BEEN A LONG TIME...

FINALLY!

IT'S GINNY! SHE WANTS TO COME OVER. YOU'RE NOT "BUSY" RIGHT NOW, SO I WENT AHEAD AND SAID YES.

GINNY?

IT WILL BE *SO* NICE TO SEE YOU PLAYING AGAIN WITH—

GINNY?!

YES, *GINNY*. SHE'S BEEN CALLING ALL SUMMER! I THINK SHE WANTS TO MAKE UP WITH YOU, SO I SUGGEST YOU AT LEAST BE *NICE* TO HER, *OK?*

GOOD *GRIEF.* THANKS A *LOT,* MOM. REAL HELPFUL.

OK.

151

A week later, I wake up on the first day of school, and I am excited!

WONDERFUL WORK, CECE!

A NEW TEACHER!

7×2
2×7
4)754

A+

609

COOL NEW SCHOOL SUPPLIES!

CECE, CAN YOU HELP ME WITH MY MATH?

YOU PLUS ME EQUALS *US*, BABY!

CUTE NEW BOYFRIEND?

BUT WAIT A MINUTE! I ONLY WEAR THIS GIANT THING AT *SCHOOL*—

—WHICH MEANS THAT *MIKE MILLER* HAS NEVER SEEN THE PHONIC EAR BEFORE! NO *WAY* IS HE *EVER* GONNA LIKE ME NOW!

YOU LOOK *WEIRD!* I'LL ASK SOME *OTHER GIRL* ABOUT THE MATH...

WHAT!?

The first day back at school is always difficult: I have to walk past everyone's desk to give my new teacher the microphone.

If there's one thing I hate, it's showing the microphone to a teacher for the first time...

...mostly because everyone stares at me as I go up to the teacher's desk.

And today, *Mike Miller* is staring at me, too!

I WISH HE COULDN'T SEE MY CORDS! HE MUST THINK I'M A TOTAL *WEIRDO!*

MRS. SINKLEMANN, THIS IS THE MICROPHONE. AND HERE'S WHAT YOU DO...

154

Actually, it's totally worth giving Mrs. Sinklemann the microphone each day. Otherwise, I would miss out on all the fun. She's an awesome teacher...

I'VE GOT A GIRL NAMED BONEY MALONEY...

SHE'S AS SKINNY AS A PIECE OF MACARONI!

...and her classroom is *the* place to be.

I'M SO THRILLED TO SHARE MY BUTTERFLIES WITH ALL OF YOU!

But one day during storytime, I realize that Mrs. Sinklemann is looking kinda fuzzy.

...HIS FLESH IS ROTTING OFF THOSE MEAN BONES, AND MAGGOTS ARE CREEPING IN HIS EYE SOCKETS AND CRAWLING OUT HIS NOSE HOLES...

And the kids look kinda fuzzy, too. Could it be love that's making my eyes all blurry?

"THAT'S A LIE, THAT'S A DISGUSTING LIE," TURTLE SHOUTED.

The blurriness gets worse. And now I have a serious problem!

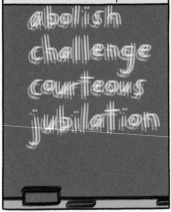

abolish
challenge
courteous
jubilation

We're taking a vocabulary test today, and I can't read the words that we're supposed to define!

ARE THOSE EVEN *WORDS*?!

I want to ask Mrs. Sinklemann for help, but where is she?

Oh!—I can *hear* her! And it sounds like she's talking to another teacher:

BAD DAY, MRS. WEST?

OH, THOSE **BRATS!** THEY'RE GONNA SEND ME TO AN EARLY GRAVE!

HMMM. THAT MEANS SHE'S NOT EVEN IN THE ROOM! I BET SHE'S IN THE TEACHERS' LOUNGE!

HEY, GINNY!

WHAT'S THE FIRST WORD ON THE BOARD? I CAN'T SEE IT! EVERYTHING'S SO BLURRY!

SHHHH!

Everyone's staring at me—*again!*—and for once I wish it *was* hearing-aid related!

WAH!

THERE, THERE. GO GET A DRINK OF WATER, AND TRY TO SETTLE DOWN.

DID *MIKE MILLER* ACTUALLY SEE ME *CRYING?* I BET HE THINKS I'M A *BIG BABY!*

WHY DIDN'T MRS. SINKLEMANN GIVE ME A CHANCE TO EXPLAIN?

AND NOW SHE'S TREATING ME LIKE A *CHEATER!* AND OH NO! *MOM AND DAD!* WHAT WILL I TELL *THEM?* AND WILL *THEY* BELIEVE ME?

I return to my classroom, but before I open the door, I listen.

IT SOUNDS LIKE MRS. SINKLEMANN IS DOING MATH NOW. I GUESS IT'S SAFE TO GO BACK IN...

I HOPE NO ONE'S LOOKING AT ME! I CAN'T EVEN *SEE* IF ANYONE'S LOOKING AT ME!

I get home before Mom does. And when she arrives, I am ready...

UH...MOM?

OH, HI!

UM, I SAW MRS. SINKLEMANN JUST TEN MINUTES AGO AT THE GREEN MARKET. SHE TOLD ME WHAT HAPPENED. I KNEW YOU'D BE UPSET, SO I BOUGHT YOU SOMETHING...

HERE YA GO.

OH, MAMA! A HOSTESS PIE! AND *CHERRY*, EVEN!

WANT TO TELL ME WHAT HAPPENED?

fourteen

Sure enough, Mom is right. On Saturday, I get glasses—and they are *incredible*.

The faraway stuff that had been so blurry? It's all so much clearer now!

We eat out that day, and at the restaurant I discover that my glasses make everyone's mouths clearer, too—even faraway mouths. I can lip-read like never before.

BLURRY...

CLEAR...

BLURRY...

CLEAR—HEY! IT'S *MARTHA!*

MAYBE I CAN IMPRESS HER WITH MY NEW GLASSES!

SHE'LL *LOVE 'EM!*

ZOWIE! THESE *SPELLBINDING SPECTACLES* CAN SPOT MY SIDEKICK FROM MORE THAN A MILE AWAY! AND JUST WAIT TILL SHE YIELDS TO THEIR *HYPNOTIC CHARMS!*

164

On Monday morning, I go to the bus stop wearing my brand-new glasses.

HEY! YOU GOT GLASSES!

C'MON, MARTHA, CHECK 'EM OUT! I'M KINDA LIKE HELEN KELLER "LITE" NOW, HEH HEH!

BLEH!

EW!

MARTHA, *WAIT!* THE GLASSES HAVE NOTHING TO DO WITH WHAT HAPPENED TO MY EYE! *HONEST!*

fifteen

I love my glasses. Being able to see makes everything easier—especially at school.

OH! *NOW* I GET IT!

90° right angle

NEVER, N

So I decide to really, really study.

AH! KNOWLEDGE IS POWER!

Maybe if I make good grades, here's what will happen:

DO YOU KNOW CECE?

YOU MEAN THAT *DEAF KID?*

NO! I MEAN THE *SMARTEST* KID IN THE *WHOLE SCHOOL!*

My hard work pays off in all my classes...

CECELIA BELL	GRADE 5	SINKLEMANN	
ENGLISH	A	MUSIC	S
MATH	A	ART	S
SOC. STUDIES	A		
SCIENCE	A	PHYS. ED.	
L. Sinklemann		Parent Signature	

...except one: Physical Education, also known as P.E.

NOT SATISFACTORY?! *WHAT?!!*

Well, I know I'm not very athletic...

OOF!

OW!

NO *WAY* CAN I HIT *THAT!*

...and it's so hard to know what to do when everybody's yelling different things at me.

BLAH WAH!

MEEMEEE!

TOE *DABAW* AH *EEBA!*

OOGA!

The P.E. teacher, Mr. Potts, doesn't help my situation at all. In fact, I live in fear of him!

AWRIGHT, KIDS! LET'S BREAK IT UP INTO *TWO TEAMS* FOR SOME *MAJOR KICKBALL ACTION!*

UH...DON'T FORGET THE MICROPHONE, MR. POTTS...

And he really *does* treat us as if we are two separate teams: the athletic kids...

Y'ALL ARE AWESOME!

...and everyone else.

HAR! GOOD LUCK!

Luckily, we don't have P.E. every day. But today we do—and we're playing *kickball*.

I GUESS I'LL TAKE CECE...

AT LEAST I GOT CALLED BEFORE HENRY FOR ONCE!

Kickball is a disaster. Whether I'm kicking...

MISSED—AGAIN!

...or trying to throw the ball—I *know* I stink.

BBETT!

NN OOO

NA

HOOGA

AH WOO BAH! OH ETT EEAH!

WO

BAW

CHA

FIBBA

WARD

BA DO A!

AMMA O

BLAH WUM

OBB GOBBA BAW!

SHAW BAH MO

I sneak in a little break during the game, and suddenly, I hear Mr. Potts talking to himself.

DANG MICROPHONE'S ALL TANGLED UP IN MY WHISTLE! I'LL JUST—OOPS!

PHYS ED

OH *NO!*

170

I watch as the microphone falls toward the Hardest Surface in the Known Universe—the gym floor!

WHOOPSIE! HEH HEH...

WHOOPSIE?! IS THAT ALL YOU'VE GOT?

It's broken! Mr. Potts *broke* my microphone!

CRACKLEZZZZZZZCRINKLECRAC... ZZ CRAKKKKK ZZZZZZZZ ZZZZZZZZ

HELLO? HELLO?

TESTING, 1-2-3...

HELLO?

I don't understand *anything* now. Mrs. Sinklemann seems so far away...

SO WHEN WE OOGA MOO, WE MUMBLE BLAH GAH!

bear
bare
read read
red reed

NEVER, N...

?

...and she never stays still. Even with my glasses, I can barely see enough to lip-read.

I SAW MOOLEE OOMA! MOOLEE OOMA HEY, HEY...

?

Thank goodness Mrs. Sinklemann is sympathetic.

I WROTE DOWN YOUR HOMEWORK... IT'LL BE BETTER TOMORROW, I BET!

SNIFF!

I'm still kinda worried, though.

CECELIA BELL   GRADE 5   SINKLEMANN

ENGLISH	F	MUSIC	
MATH	F		NS
SOC. ST...ES	F	ART	
ENG...	F		NS
		PHYS. ED.	
		Parent Signature	NS

WHAT'S GONNA HAPPEN?

When I get home, I put on my behind-the-ear aids, and I show Mom the broken microphone. She calls my audiologist.

...UH-HUH, I SEE. SILVER SPRING, *MARYLAND*? OK, LET ME GET A PENCIL...

WE'RE SENDING THE MICROPHONE AND YOUR HEARING AID TO MARYLAND. I GUESS YOU'LL HAVE TO WEAR YOUR BEHIND-THE-EAR AIDS TO SCHOOL FOR A WHILE.

FOR HOW LONG?

UM...EVERYTHING WILL COME BACK TO US IN THE MAIL IN FOUR TO SIX WEEKS.

FOUR TO SIX *WEEKS*!?

I WON'T BE ABLE TO UNDERSTAND *ANYTHING*! I'LL FAIL *EVERYTHING*!

WHAT AM I GONNA *DO?*

FOUR TO SIX *WEEKS* WITHOUT MY *SUPERPOWERS?* I DON'T KNOW WHAT *I'M* GONNA DO, EITHER—BUT IT AIN'T GONNA BE PRETTY!

The next morning, for the first time ever, I actually *miss* putting on the Phonic Ear.

I FEEL SO... SO *NAKED!*

I GUESS I SHOULD BE HAPPY TO HAVE THESE AIDS. BUT HOW AM I GONNA UNDERSTAND MRS. SINKLEMANN? I'M NOT *THAT* GOOD AT LIP-READING!

At school...

BLAH BLAH WAH MUMWAH HOO. AN ATTS EE ENN!

ARGH! I CAN'T FOLLOW THE BOOK IF SHE'S COVERING HER FACE WITH IT! AND I THINK I JUST MISSED THE ENDING! OH, *FOUR TO SIX WEEKS?* OF *THIS?*

Later that day... MRS. SINKLEMANN TOLD *ME* TO TELL *YOOO* THAT WE'VE GOT PEE-EE NEXT.

YEAH. I KNOW.

AND I AM *READY.*

WITH OR WITHOUT SUPERPOWERS, I AM STILL *EL DEAFO*— AND I AM *OUTRAGED!*

Today in P.E., we are supposed to do tests for the Presidential Physical Fitness Award.

HE SAYS THE GIRLS HAVE TO DO "FLEXED-ARM HANGS" LIKE BECK-Y IS DO-ING!

YIKES.

A flexed-arm hang means you have to stay in a pull-up position and keep your chin over the bar for as long as you can stand it!

00:10

00:02

00:23

Now it's my turn.

ALRIGHT, *BELL*. LET'S SEE WHAT *YOU* CAN DO, HEH.

LOOK OUT, *POTTS*! PREPARE TO BE *AMAZED*!

Our hero is suddenly fueled by rage!

THAT MAN HAS COST ME MY SUPERPOWERS...

00:20

...MY GOOD GRADES...

00:40

...BUT *NOT* MY GOOD NAME!

00:64

SIXTY-FOUR SECONDS! I AM *EL DEAFO!* I AM A *CHAMPION!*

It's a world record! The president of the United States of America himself arrives to present El Deafo with her hard-earned award!

MOVE OVER, *POTTS!*

OUR GREAT NATION PRESENTS THIS PHYSICAL FITNESS AWARD TO YOU, EL DEAFO, FOR YOUR REMARKABLE FEATS OF SKILL AND TALENT!

sixteen

THE SUSPENSE IS KILLING ME!

WHOA! THAT'S NOT A PHONIC EAR— IT'S A PENCIL! A *CURLY* PENCIL!

GEE, DAD! A CURLY PENCIL! I'VE NEVER SEEN ANYTHING LIKE IT! IT'S *AWESOME!* THANKS, DAD!

GLAD YOU LIKE IT!

OH MAN! IT WRITES LIKE A REAL PENCIL, TOO! THAT IS *SO COOL!*

I do the rest of my homework with my new curly pencil, even though it takes a whole lot longer.

I CAN'T WAIT TO SHOW THIS TO EVERYBODY AT SCHOOL TOMORROW!

When I wake up the next morning, I don't have the usual sinking feeling that I've had every day since the Phonic Ear broke. Instead, I am excited!

I dress quickly...

GO, GO, GO!

...I eat quickly...

GO, GO, GO!

GOOD GRIEF!

...and I hurry out the door.

GO, GO, GO!

WAIT! DON'T FORGET YOUR LUNCH MONEY!

JUST WAIT TILL THE KIDS AT THE BUS STOP SEE *THIS!* MAYBE EVEN *MARTHA* WILL BE IMPRESSED!

Shoot. Martha's not here yet. But Mike is!

HEY! LOOK WHAT I GOT!

TA-DA!

WOW!

NEAT!

MY DAD GAVE THIS TO ME. YOU CAN HOLD IT, BUT BE CAREFUL! IT COULD BREAK, JUST LIKE A REAL PENCIL CAN!

CAREFUL!

182

SNIFFLE...

WAH!

I CAN'T *BELIEVE* THIS! I'M IN THE *FIFTH GRADE* AND I'M *BAWLING* IN FRONT OF *EVERYBODY*! IN FRONT OF MIKE MILLER!—AGAIN!

BWAH—WAH!

CECE?

UH...UH...

MAMA!

184

185

When I get to school, I go to the gym like always and sit in the bleachers. But no *way* am I sitting with the neighborhood kids—or any other kids, for that matter.

I stare straight ahead and try not to cry anymore.

But suddenly, out of the corner of my eye, I see somebody coming—it's *Johnnie!* And he's being pushed toward me by *MIKE MILLER!*

OK, JOHNNIE. *APOLOGIZE.*

UH, SORRY ABOUT THE PENCIL.

UH...

I DON'T KNOW *WHAT* TO FEEL...

UM, LISTEN. I'M SORRY ABOUT WHAT HAPPENED. IT WAS A REALLY COOL PENCIL. I DON'T KNOW WHY HE FELT LIKE HE HAD TO DO THAT!

...SHOULD I FEEL HAPPINESS, BECAUSE MIKE MILLER REALLY *IS* NICE AND MIGHT ACTUALLY CARE ABOUT ME?

UH...

OR *SHAME*, BECAUSE *MIKE MILLER* WITNESSED THE WHOLE THING...

UH...

WELL, I GOTTA GO...

...AND HE JUST FEELS *SORRY* FOR ME AND MY WHOLE *CRYBABY DEAF KID* SELF?

BYE. HOPE YOU FEEL BETTER.

AND NOW HE'S GONE. *MIKE MILLER* WAS SITTING RIGHT HERE BESIDE ME, AND I NEVER SAID A WORD! RATS.

BYE.

seventeen

Anyway, most of us work while Mrs. Sinklemann is gone...

...but sometimes, a few of us don't.

HEY, MIKE! CATCH!

WHOOP!

Sometimes the "bad" kids remember to watch the door for Mrs. Sinklemann.

GOD BLESS MY UNDERWEAR, THEY'RE THE O-NLY PAIR I HAVE! STAND BESIDE THEM, AND GUIDE THEM...

UH-OH...

But sometimes, like today, they forget.

SLAM!

CHILDREN! JUST *WHAT* IS GOING ON HERE? BACK TO YOUR SEATS— RIGHT *NOW!*

BETTER LOOK BUSY!

Uh-oh. Mrs. Sinklemann stands in front of her giant apple painted on the blackboard.

I AM *SO* DISAPPOINTED.

PAUL, J.P., MIKE, BECKY, MANDY— I'M WRITING *YOUR* NAMES IN THE APPLE...

...AND AS YOU KNOW, *A FEW ROTTEN SPOTS SPOIL THE WHOLE THING.* *GOODNESS.* LET'S PUT OUR THINGS AWAY AND GET READY FOR LUNCH.

MIKE SURE LOOKS EMBARRASSED. I WISH I COULD TALK TO HIM AND MAKE HIM FEEL BETTER. BUT HE PROBABLY THINKS I'M A BIG CRYBABY AFTER THIS MORNING.

UGH! JUST *TALK,* CECE!

UH...MIKE?

YEAH?

eighteen

Every day after school, I ask Mom the same question, and I get the same answer:

IS IT HERE YET?

NOT YET.

IS IT HERE YET?

NOT YET.

IS IT HERE YET?

NOT YET.

Until finally, after four weeks and three days of waiting...

IS IT—

YES!

OH BOY!

OH, MY *PRECIOUS!* HOW COULD I HAVE *EVER* BEEN ASHAMED OF YOU? LIFE HAS BEEN A *MESS* WITHOUT YOU AND THE MICROPHONE!

The next day at school, I am actually happy to be holding the microphone as I walk past everyone.

OH, IT'S BACK! HOW LOVELY!

TESTING, 1-2-3...

TESTING, 1-2-3...

CECE, CAN YOU HEAR ME A LITTLE BETTER NOW?

YES!

ALRIGHTY, TURN YOUR MATH BOOKS TO PAGE 153 FOR FRACTIONS AND THEN SOLVE

NOW THAT I CAN HEAR AND UNDERSTAND MRS. SINKLEMANN AGAIN, SCHOOL'S GONNA BE A BREEZE!

My day gets even better when Mrs. Sinklemann makes this announcement:

AS YOU MAY KNOW, THE SIXTH-GRADERS ARE GIVING A PRESENTATION CALLED "THE WONDERFUL WORLD OF BOOKS." IT'S A BIG PART OF OUR SCHOOL-WIDE "READING IS FUN" CAMPAIGN.

THE SIXTH-GRADE TEACHERS HAVE REQUESTED TWO FIFTH-GRADERS "ON THE SMALLISH SIDE" TO POSE AS GIANT BOOKENDS ON THE STAGE DURING THE PRESENTATION.

THE FIRST STUDENT I'VE SELECTED IS... CECE BELL!

REALLY!? I GET TO BE ON STAGE AND EVERYTHING? WOW!

AND THE SECOND STUDENT I'VE SELECTED—A BOY—IS...

A BOY?! MIKE IS KINDA SHORT. COULD IT BE?

MIKE MILLER!

IT IS!

CECE AND MIKE— I WILL LET YOUR MOMS KNOW...

...AS THEY'LL NEED TO GET YOU SOME MATCHING PAJAMAS.

HEE HEE HEE!

WHAT!? MATCHING *PAJAMAS?* IN FRONT OF THE *WHOLE SCHOOL?* AND NO *WAY* AM I "ON THE SMALLISH SIDE"!

I DON'T WANT TO WEAR PAJAMAS IN FRONT OF THE WHOLE SCHOOL, EITHER. HOWEVER...

MIKE MILLER. IN PAJAMAS.

THIS COULD GET *EMBARRASSING.*

A few days later, after school...

WELL, HI! LISTEN, DON'T START YOUR HOMEWORK YET. WE'RE GOING TO THE MILLERS' HOUSE TO GET THE PAJAMAS THAT MRS. MILLER BOUGHT FOR YOU!

MIKE MILLER'S HOUSE?!

HI, NANCY!

COME ON IN!

OK. HERE ARE CECE'S PAJAMAS...

SO PRECIOUS!

RUFFLES?!

...AND HERE ARE MIKE'S PAJAMAS!

ADORABLE!

MOM!

ADORABLE...

UH, THOSE PAJAMAS ARE KINDA GOOFY, DON'T YOU THINK?

UH...YEAH...

I'LL LOOK GOOFY. HE'LL LOOK SO CUTE!

On the morning of the presentation, there's an announcement over the loudspeaker.

BLAH OO WAH... MEEMEE ELUM WAH WAH... BA WUBBA AH WAH BLAH... GAH SUMN O EE BLAH WAH GOOAH BLAH LAH OO WAH EN MEEMEE...

CLASS, WE'LL BE GOING TO THE GYM IN TWENTY MINUTES. MIKE AND CECE, YOU GO ON AHEAD...

THAT'S US. YOU READY?

"US"? OH YES!

We grab our pajamas and silently head to the restrooms to change. Well, *almost* silently. Thanks to the Phonic Ear, I can still hear Mrs. Sinklemann talking to our class.

CLASS...LET'S LINE UP AND GET READY FOR THE PRESENTATION. REMEMBER... POLITE TO... SIXTH GR...

BOYS

GIRLS

THIS IS NUTS.

UH... WOW.

BOYS

GIRLS

197

All the classes file in. The sixth-graders start singing. Mike and I sit. And sit. And sit. Suddenly, I hear something weird...

OOGA LOO MA GOOGA MOOO, AN LALA MA GA WAH...

THE Wonderful World OF BOOKS!

...and it ain't singing!

*tinkle *tinkle *tinkle

HAAAAAAAAAAAAAAH...

WOCKA WOCKA

SWEET RELIEF.

HEE HEE!

FLUSH!

HA HA! SNORT!

I HAVE GOT TO STOP LAUGHING!

198

The presentation ends. The sixth-graders take a bow, and so do we.

I SEE MRS. SINKLEMANN HAS COME BACK. HOPE SHE HAD FUN IN THE POTTY! OH! I *GOTTA* STOP GIGGLING!

CLAP CLAP

CLAP CLAP

A few minutes later, we change into our regular clothes and head back to class.

I HOPE I *NEVER* SEE THESE PAJAMAS AGAIN! LET'S JUST LEAVE THEM HERE IN THE BAGS.

UH...OK.

I HOPE I *DO* SEE THOSE PAJAMAS AGAIN!

SO...*UMM.* WHAT WERE YOU GIGGLING ABOUT UP THERE?

SHOULD I TELL HIM? I'VE NEVER TALKED TO *ANYONE* ABOUT THIS STUFF. AND I CAN'T EVEN *BEGIN* TO TALK TO *HIM.* I WISH I REALLY *DID* HAVE SUPERPOWERS! THEN IT WOULD ALL BE SO *EASY!*

UM...UH...YOU ASKED WHAT I WAS GIGGLING ABOUT EARLIER. WELL... I HAVE AN AMAZING ABILITY!

HUH?

I AM *FINALLY* TALKING TO HIM!

YOU KNOW THAT MICROPHONE MRS. SINKLEMANN WEARS? AND—AHEM—THIS THING THAT I WEAR?

YEAH?

WELL, SOMEHOW THEY WORK TOGETHER TO HELP ME HEAR MRS. SINKLEMANN BETTER. AND THEY ARE SO POWERFUL...

...THAT I CAN HEAR MRS. SINKLEMANN WHEREVER SHE IS IN THE *ENTIRE SCHOOL BUILDING!*

NO WAY!

SO, DURING THE PRESENTATION... GUESS WHAT I HEARD?

WHAT?

I HEARD MRS. SINKLEMANN... *PEEING!!!*

FOR *REAL?!*

nineteen

EL DEAFO'S FIRST DATE

FOR YOU, MY DARLING, SWEET CHOCOLATES...

POUR MOI?

...AND A SINGLE ROSE. ITS BEAUTY SHALL NE'ER SURPASS THAT OF THE ONE YOU WEAR UPON YOUR BREAST!

DID HE JUST SAY "BREAST"?

NOW KISS ME!

Smooch!

SEE YA SOON! AND WEAR *THAT* HEARING AID—BRING THE MICROPHONE, TOO!

HMM...THAT'S NOT *QUITE* WHAT I HAD IN MIND...

I take my school stuff home and then head right over to Mike's house.

HI!

HEY! OH, GOOD! YOU'VE GOT THE MICROPHONE!

I WANNA DO A LITTLE EXPERIMENT. *I'LL* WEAR THE MICROPHONE AND WALK DOWNTOWN. *YOU* STAY HERE. *I'LL* TALK THE WHOLE TIME, AND *YOU* CAN LISTEN. THEN WE'LL KNOW JUST HOW STRONG THIS THING REALLY IS!

WHAT D'YA THINK?

OK, I GUESS!

TESTING, TESTING, CAN YOU HEAR ME?

TESTING, TESTING, CAN YOU HEAR ME?

YEP!

Mike heads downtown, and I listen.

KNOW YOU CAN PROBABLY STILL SEE ME I'M AT DAN'S HOUSE

THIS IS A REALLY WEIRD "*DATE*"...

..NOW I'M CROSSING THE STREET AT DAVID'S HOUSE...TESTING, 1-2, TESTING, TEST

BUT I'LL TAKE IT!

I keep listening... ....ARE YOU STILL THERE, CECE? NOW I'M IN FRONT O TRICIA'S HOUSE...I'M GONNA KEEP ON GOING DOWNTO

I GOTTA ADMIT, THIS IS PRETTY NEAT! EVEN *I* DIDN'T KNOW IT COULD GO *THAT FAR!*

Minutes pass. Then Suzie, a neighborhood kid, appears.

HEY, CECE! WHATCHA DOIN'?

SHOULD I TELL HER? I TOLD MIKE MILLER, AND HE WAS OK WITH IT...

I CAN TELL OTHER PEOPLE TOO—RIGHT?

I decide to take a chance. I explain the whole thing to Suzie. And she says:

SERIOUSLY?! THAT'S *AMAZING!* WHERE IS MIKE NOW?

...NOW I'M AT THE BIG BAPTIST CHURCH...AND

AT THE BIG BAPTIST CHURCH!

A few more minutes pass, and Suzie's friend Helen appears.

WHAT'S GOING ON?

GET *THIS!* MIKE IS WEARING CECE'S MICROPHONE THING AND HE'S WALKING DOWNTOWN AND TALKING, AND SHE CAN HEAR IT ALL!

WHAT'S HAPPENING?

IT'S SO COOL! CECE IS LISTENING TO MIKE...

WHERE IS HE NOW?

PAWN SHOP A T ME! I T AZY! AND MY LF! TESTIN NG SURE

THIS IS A LITTLE EMBARRASSING. BUT HECK! THEY THINK I'M *COOL!*

WHAT'S HE SAYING?

And then *another* kid shows up. But not just any kid—it's *Martha!*

WHAT'S EVERYBODY DOING?

MIKE'S USING CECE'S MICROPHONE THING AND HE'S TALKING TO HER WHILE HE WALKS DOWNTOWN!

SHE CAN HEAR EVERYTHING HE SAYS!

HE'S AT THE PAWN SHOP *RIGHT NOW!*

STICK AROUND! CECE'S BEEN TELLING US WHERE HE IS AND WHAT HE SAYS!

UH...

PLEASE STAY!

UMM...I GOTTA GO PICK UP SOME STUFF FOR MY MOM AT THE GREEN MARKET.

IT *DOES* KINDA SOUND LIKE FUN.

ACKLEZZZNOW I'M E CORNER OF BROA ZZZZZZZRPZ

PLEASE STAY PLEASE STAY PLEASE STAY *PLEASE!*

ZZZZZZZ POPZZZZZZZZZCRRZZZZZC ZZZZZZZZZCRRCK

BUT I GOTTA GO.

RATS...

RATS. WELL, AT LEAST SHE *TALKED* TO ME FOR ONCE...

CECE?

UM, I DIDN'T REALLY BELIEVE YOU AT FIRST, BUT OUR EXPERIMENT PROVED IT! THIS THING IS *STRONG!*

YEP.

...AND HECK, *MIKE MILLER* IS TALKING TO ME *NOW!*

THAT WAS FUN! MAYBE WE CAN HAVE EVEN *MORE* FUN WITH IT AT SCHOOL!

FUN? WHAT KIND OF FUN?

I DUNNO. BUT I'LL THINK OF *SOMETHING!*

HMM. SOUNDS LIKE *TROUBLE.* AND I SURE DON'T WANT TO BE A ROTTEN SPOT ON MRS. SINKLEMANN'S APPLE!

BUT FOR *MIKE MILLER,* I'D DO ALMOST ANYTHING...

WELL— SEE YA!

...AFTER ALL, THANKS TO HIS "EXPERIMENT," THE NEIGHBORHOOD KIDS THINK I'M *COOL*...

...AND MARTHA SPOKE TO ME...

...AND—*GEE!* HE'S AN ABSOLUTE *DREAMBOAT!*

BYE!

210

twenty

The next morning on the bus, I save a seat for Martha.

I JUST *KNOW* I CAN CONVINCE HER TO BE FRIENDS AGAIN!

HEY, CECE! IS THIS SEAT TAKEN?

UH...

HOW CAN I SAY NO?

YOU KNOW WHAT I KEEP THINKING ABOUT?

ME?

YOUR HEARING AID AND THAT MICROPHONE! THEY'RE SO COOL!

COOL!? WOW! BUT DOES HE THINK *I'M* COOL, TOO?

SO...I'VE GOT A PLAN. WHEN MRS. SINKLEMANN LEAVES TODAY FOR QUIET MATH, YOU CAN USE YOUR STUFF TO LISTEN OUT FOR HER. WE CAN ALL HAVE FUN UNTIL YOU TELL US SHE'S COMING BACK! YOU'LL BE A *HERO!* WHAT D'YA SAY?

UM... SURE!

Once I'm at school, though, I'm not so sure about Mike's big plan. I can't concentrate on anything, not even on what Mrs. Sinklemann is saying.

WHAT HAVE I JUST AGREED TO DO? AND WHAT IF IT DOESN'T WORK? AND—*OH!*—WHAT IF I GET IN *BIG TROUBLE?*

MIKE AND THE NEIGHBORHOOD KIDS THINK MY HEARING AID IS COOL—BUT WHAT IF MY CLASSMATES DON'T THINK SO?

WILL I BE A HERO? OR WILL I BE *HUMILIATED?*

Suddenly, Mrs. Sinklemann's voice is all too clear:

CLASS, IT'S TIME TO PUT YOUR ART THINGS AWAY. QUIET MATH IS STARTING SOON!

BE GOOD, EVERYONE! I'LL BE BACK IN TWENTY MINUTES!

WHAT!? ALREADY?

I hear the tap of Mrs. Sinklemann's shoes as she goes up the stairs. Can I really do what Mike wants me to do?

TAP TAP TAP...

OK, EVERYBODY...

LET'S PARTY!

NO *WAY!* I DON'T WANNA BE A ROTTEN SPOT AGAIN!

ME, NEITHER!

DON'T WORRY! ME AND CECE HAVE A PLAN!

OH *YEAH?* WHAT IS IT?

CECE'S HEARING AID LETS HER HEAR MRS. SINKLEMANN WHEREVER SHE IS IN THE *WHOLE BUILDING!* SO CECE'S GONNA LISTEN OUT FOR HER AND TELL US WHEN SHE'S COMING BACK! WE CAN SNEAK BACK TO OUR DESKS—AND MRS. SINKLEMANN WILL NEVER HAVE TO KNOW!

OH BOY. WHAT'S EVERYBODY GONNA THINK OF ME *NOW?*

I wait for someone—anyone—to say something.

And then suddenly, someone does:

YOU CAN *DO* THAT?

WHERE IS SHE *RIGHT NOW?*

SHE'S IN THE TEACHERS' LOUNGE! I CAN HEAR HER PUFFING ON A CIGARETTE!

THIS PLAN IS *TOTALLY* GONNA WORK!

IT'S PARTY TIME!

BUT HURRY! WE'VE ONLY GOT ABOUT FIFTEEN MINUTES!

My classmates are having the time of their lives. I think about joining them, but I've got an important job to do. So I watch—and I listen.

Ten minutes later...

UM...CAN YOU STILL HEAR HER? I MEAN, LIKE, WHERE IS MRS. SINKLEMANN NOW?

WELL—AHEM— SHE'S IN THE *BATHROOM!*

NO *WAY!!!* THAT'S *HILARIOUS!* HEY, EVERYBODY! CECE CAN HEAR MRS. SINKLEMANN USING THE *BATHROOM!*

YOU CAN *HEAR* THAT? *SERIOUSLY?* THAT'S *AWESOME!*

GEE, I WISH *I* HAD A HEARING AID, TOO!

IT'S *CRAZY!* FOR SO LONG, I'VE WISHED THAT *I* COULD HEAR LIKE *THEY* DO. BUT *I* HAVE SOMETHING *THEY* DON'T HAVE—*SUPERPOWERS!* AND IT'S ACTUALLY *FUN* TO SHARE THEM LIKE THIS!

TAP TAP TAP...

BUT *WAIT!* WHERE IS MRS. SINKLEMANN NOW?

TAP
TAP

GOING DOWNSTAIRS

THIS CAN ONLY MEAN ONE THING: MRS. SINKLEMANN'S *COMING BACK!*

And now I have to warn my classmates that she's headed our way!

TIME IS RUNNING OUT! IT'S NOW OR NEVER! TELL THEM!

TAP TAP

But I *never* do stuff like this! I could get in so much trouble!

SO WHAT!? THIS IS YOUR PART OF THE PLAN!

TAP TAP

YOUR CLASSMATES NEED *YOUR HELP.* BE A HERO!

TAP TAP

STAND UP! SHOUT IT OUT! TELL THEM!

We get back to our seats just in time.

HOW LOVELY! I SEE THAT THERE ARE NO ROTTEN SPOTS FOR THE APPLE TODAY!

WE DID IT! I DID IT!

PSST! THAT WAS *SO COOL!* HOW COME YOU NEVER TOLD *ME* YOU COULD DO THAT?

UH...I DUNNO.

IS IT MY IMAGINATION, OR IS GINNY *FINALLY* TALKING TO ME IN A NORMAL WAY? THERE'S HOPE FOR US YET!

OH. WELL, IT'S NEAT!

UM, ANYWAY...MIKE TOLD ME TO TELL YOU THAT HE WAS RIGHT! YOU'RE A *HERO!*

OF *COURSE* I'M A HERO— I AM *EL DEAFO!*

twenty-one

The next morning, during a brief recess before Quiet Math, we come up with a new plan.

I BROUGHT MY QUEEN RECORD! WE CAN PLAY IT TODAY DURING QUIET MATH! LIKE A *REAL* PARTY, WITH MUSIC!

I'LL LISTEN OUT FOR US AGAIN!

UH...GUYS? MRS. SINKLEMANN WANTS US OVER AT THE RUG...

We take our seats on the rug...

IT'S CRAZY! YESTERDAY I WAS SCARED TO DO THE PLAN. TODAY I'M *EXCITED!*

...and then Mrs. Sinklemann makes an announcement.

CLASS, WE'RE DOING SOMETHING SPECIAL TODAY. SO YOU'LL BE HAPPY TO HEAR THAT THIS MEANS THERE WILL BE NO QUIET MATH!

AWWWWWWWWWW!

MY GOODNESS! I HAD *NO IDEA* THAT YOU ALL ENJOY QUIET MATH SO MUCH! HOW *LOVELY!*

IT'S TIME FOR MORE OF OUR "READING IS FUN" CAMPAIGN! OUR GUIDANCE COUNSELOR, MRS. CATAWBA, IS GOING TO VISIT US THIS MORNING. SHE'LL BE SHARING HER FAVORITE BOOK WITH YOU—

—AND, OH! HERE SHE IS, RIGHT NOW!

HELLO, CHILDREN!

TODAY WE WILL BE READING FROM THIS WONDERFUL BOOK, *T.A. FOR TOTS.* IT DESCRIBES FEELINGS IN SUCH A CUTE WAY!

GROAN. I'VE SEEN THIS BOOK BEFORE. SO CORNY.

HERE'S HOW IT WORKS: IF SOMEONE SAYS SOMETHING NICE TO YOU, OR GIVES YOU A HUG, YOU FEEL GOOD, RIGHT? THAT FEELING IS A *WARM FUZZY!*

BUT THAT FEELING YOU GET WHEN SOMEONE IS MEAN TO YOU, OR HURTS YOU? THAT'S A *COLD PRICKLY!* BRRRRRR!

TODAY WE'LL BE MAKING OUR OWN WARM FUZZIES OUT OF POM-POM BALLS!

AND COLD PRICKLIES, TOO? I WANNA MAKE ONE OF *THOSE!*

GOODNESS, NO! NOW, GO BACK TO YOUR DESKS, AND I'LL PASS OUT THE MATERIALS...

Here's what we get:

GLUE

Felt →

pom-pom balls

googly eyes

YOU'LL ALL BE GETTING ONE OF THESE PAPER BAGS, TOO. I WANT YOU TO PERSONALIZE IT. MAKE IT *YOU!*

ONCE YOU'VE MADE YOUR BAG AND SOME WARM FUZZIES, YOU'LL EXCHANGE FUZZIES WITH YOUR FRIENDS. YOU CAN KEEP YOUR FUZZIES IN YOUR BAG—AND YOU'LL FEEL GOOD ALL DAY!

STILL PRETTY CORNY— BUT AT LEAST WE GET TO *MAKE* SOMETHING!

224

I know *exactly* what to do with my bag. I get some yarn, some tape, and two old spools from the craft shelves...

WHAT A CRAZY COUPLE OF DAYS IT'S BEEN!

I FEEL SO DIFFERENT ABOUT A LOT OF THINGS...

...ABOUT MIKE, AND MARTHA... MY NEIGHBORS, AND MY CLASSMATES...

...I EVEN FEEL DIFFERENT ABOUT THE PHONIC EAR!

VOILÀ! THE PHONIC EAR BAG!

PHONIC EAR

AND ON THE BACK— A TOP SECRET PICTURE OF *ME!*

EL DEAFO

NOW—ON TO THE WARM FUZZIES!

HEY, CECE! CHECK IT OUT! IT'S THE VAN HALEN LOGO!

GULP!

VAN HALEN!? THAT CRUMMY ROCK GROUP? WHAT HAPPENED TO HIM LIKING THE BEATLES? VAN HALEN? MAYBE WE'D BE BETTER OFF BEING JUST FRIENDS...

CHECK OUT THE BACK!

I'M CALLING 'EM WORM FUZZIES! GET IT? WORM?

HEE HEE!

THAT'S HILARIOUS! UM...HERE'S MINE.

IS THAT LIKE YOUR HEARING AID? THAT'S CRAZY FUNNY!

WOW! HE GETS IT! MAYBE I'LL SHOW HIM MY DRAWING OF EL DEAFO LATER—BUT I'M NOT SURE ANYONE WOULD GET THAT...

WELL! BETTER START MAKING SOME WORMS!

I'M GONNA MAKE A LOT OF THESE THINGS, 'CAUSE I WANNA GIVE *AWAY* A LOT!

HEY, GINNY! CAN I USE YOUR SCISSORS?

THIS ONE'S MY FAVORITE! MAYBE I'LL KEEP IT...

Twenty minutes later...

ALRIGHTY, EVERYONE! LEAVE YOUR BAGS ON YOUR DESKS, GRAB YOUR FUZZIES, AND START SHARING SOME GOOD FEELINGS!

Warm Fuzzies

I try to put a warm fuzzy in as many bags as I can.

GRAB YOUR FUZZIES? HEE HEE!

And I make sure to put one in Ginny's bag...

SHE MAY BUG ME SOMETIMES...BUT SHE REALLY *IS* A GOOD FRIEND. I NEED TO BE NICER TO HER!

...and in Mike's bag, too.

I HOPE NO ONE'S LOOKING!

As corny as all that was, Mrs. Catawba was right. All those warm fuzzies make me feel really good...

...and the feeling gets me through the whole day. Even when I'm in P.E....

HI, MR. POTTS. CAREFUL!

I'M *TOTALLY* GONNA KICK THAT BALL TODAY...

...and *even* when I run into a certain person.

HEY, LAURA—LONG TIME NO SEE. WANT A WARM FUZZY?

HUH?

I pass out fuzzies on the bus ride home...

I'VE GOT SO MANY FUZZIES TO SHARE! I CAN'T WAIT TO GIVE ONE TO MOM AND DAD AND ASHLEY AND SARAH. AND I THINK I'LL GIVE MY *FAVORITE* FUZZY TO—

People can become deaf in many different ways. Some are born deaf, to either deaf or hearing parents. Some are exposed to one big, loud noise, and they lose their hearing immediately. Some might be exposed to lots of noise over a long period of time, and they lose their hearing gradually. Some might get sick with some illness or another and lose their hearing as a result of the disease.

Each deaf person also has a different *amount* of deafness—how much he or she can hear without the assistance of a hearing aid or a cochlear implant. One can be mildly deaf, moderately deaf, severely deaf, or profoundly deaf.

But more important than how the hearing loss happened, or how much hearing loss a deaf person has, is what a deaf person might choose to do with his or her hearing loss. In other words, there are lots of different ways to be deaf. And there is no right or wrong way.

Some deaf people are members of what is known as the Deaf community, also known as Deaf culture. Members of the Deaf community view their deafness as a difference, but it's a *good* difference, not a disability. Deafness is a condition that doesn't need to be fixed. Those in the Deaf community might—or might not—use hearing aids and cochlear implants to amplify sounds and speech. Sign language is the preferred means of communication in the Deaf community; Deaf people might—or might not—choose (or be able) to speak orally.

Other deaf people, however, *do* want to "fix" their hearing loss. They amplify their residual hearing with the help of hearing aids or cochlear implants. They may speak and read lips, and may or may not supplement their speech with sign language. They might think of their deafness as a difference, and they might, either secretly or openly, think of it as a disability, too.

And, I am sure, there are plenty of deaf people who would read the descriptions above and not recognize themselves at all. I am an expert on no one's deafness but my own.

I myself am "severely to profoundly" deaf, the result of a brief illness when I was four years old. While I'm fascinated by Deaf culture, I have not, as yet, pursued a direct role in it. Since I could hear and speak before I got sick, my parents were able to make decisions for me that kept me mostly in the hearing world. Their choices, and the choices that I made for myself later, helped me become pretty comfortable there. But I wasn't always so comfortable.

El Deafo is based on my childhood (and on the secret nickname I really did give myself back then). It is in no way a representation of what all deaf people might experience. It's also important to note that while I was writing and drawing the book, I was more interested in capturing the specific feelings I had as a kid with hearing loss than in being 100 percent accurate with the details. Some of the characters in the book are exactly how I remember them; others are composites of more than one person. Some of the events in the book are in the right order; others got mixed up a bit. Some of the conversations are real; others, well, ain't. But the way I *felt* as a kid—that feeling is all true. I was a deaf kid surrounded by kids who could hear. I felt different, and in my mind, being different was *not* a good thing. I secretly, *and* openly, believed that my deafness, in making me so different, was a disability. And I was ashamed.

As I grew up, however, I made some positive discoveries about deafness and about myself. I'm no longer ashamed of being deaf, nor do I think of myself as someone with a disability. I've even made peace with sign language and have a real appeciation for it. To the kid me, being deaf was a defining characteristic, one I tried to hide. Now it defines a smaller part of me, and I don't try to hide it—much. Today, I view my deafness as more of an occasional nuisance, and oddly enough, as a gift: I can turn off the sound of the world any time I want, and retreat into peaceful silence.

And being different? That turned out to be the best part of all. I found that with a little creativity, and a lot of dedication, any difference can be turned into something amazing. Our differences are our *superpowers.*

Acknowledgments

I wish there was enough room on these pages to acknowledge every friend, every family member, and every person who was nice to me at one point or another. If you are one of the above, consider yourself acknowledged, and heartily!

A lot of people helped me create this book:

Susan Van Metre believed in *El Deafo* when it was just a typed outline on two pieces of paper. She guided the book through every stage, and became a true friend along the way.

College pal David Lasky brought the book to life with his expert coloring and masterful shadow making. David's pal Frank M. Young assisted him a bit with a few of the later chapters.

Chad W. Beckerman and Katie Fitch used their estimable super-powers to put together this beautiful book. Caitlin Keegan came up with the gorgeous cover design. Sara Corbett guided the interior in the initial stages and was one of the earliest fans of the book.

Jen Graham read and reread the book so many times to get the text just right.

Sheila Keenan and Charlie Kochman shared their comics expertise.

Laura Mihalick and Jason Wells helped spread the word about *El Deafo*.

Caryn Wiseman did many things behind the scenes with positive energy and a smile.

New friend T.W. read the afterword and offered suggestions to make it better.

Emily Hemphill patiently posed for reference photos wearing the Phonic Ear and my old overalls.

Superfriend Madelyn Rosenberg was a steady source of encouragement and much-needed laughs.

And a lot of people inspired the book:

Martha Chadwick, who continues to be a true friend and soul mate.

Mike Miller, who really was that nice to me.

Emma Knight, who is my oldest friend.

Several other childhood friends, who upon reading this book might recognize bits and pieces of themselves. They might also think that they have been grossly misrepresented by my kid memories. I purposely changed their names because I know I wasn't always fair to them, in childhood or in this book. I hope they forgive me.

My classmates at Fisher School, who probably have similar stories to tell, and our teacher, Dorn Scherer, a kind soul who taught us the basics of lip-reading.

My teachers at Academy Street School and G.W. Carver Elementary School, who happily wore my microphone and treated me like all their other students.

The folks at Phonic Ear, who created the "school aid" that gave me superpowers.

Audiologists Michael Ridenhour and Dick Hawkins, who out-fitted me with my first hearing aids.

The doctors and nurses at MCV, who helped me get better.

Ashley and Sarah, who are outstanding siblings and possibly the funniest people I know.

Mom and Dad, who made all the tough decisions during what must have been a tricky time in their lives. I wish I had better words than "thank you" to express how grateful I am to both of you.

C and O, who bring me joy every day.

And Tom Angleberger, who is my truest friend of all.

Hi everybody! Yep, that's me, way back in 1975. I was finally home from the hospital, but I hadn't gotten my first hearing aid yet. My grandmother, Granny Bell, made the hat and the dress, too. I was super-crazy about that hat. Eagle-eyed readers will recognize the hat's pattern from the bathing suit featured in the book. (I can't remember exactly what that bathing suit looked like, except that it was red!)

These next few pages are chock-full of old photos of family and friends, early drawings, process pictures, and awesome art created by readers like you. I hope you'll enjoy this extra peek inside the world of El Deafo!

When I was born in 1970, I was able to hear.

Here's me with Mom and Dad.

My older brother, Ashley...

and older sister, Sarah...
soon after we moved to
Salem, Virginia, in 1976.

Here we are, all dressed up (a rare occasion!) in 1978 or so.

Ashley, Sarah, and me when we were younger. Weren't we cute?

This picture was taken around the time I got very sick with bacterial meningitis, in May of 1975. Meningitis is an infection of the spinal cord and the membranes covering the brain. It was a scary time. But there were a few bright spots...

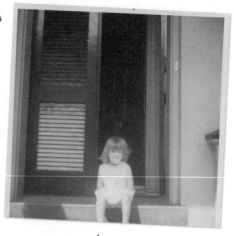

like getting this book from Sarah. It's still one of my favorites!

THE MEANEST SQUIRREL I EVER MET

by GENE ZION

Pictures by MARGARET BLOY GRAHAM

And I got Miss Bunn!

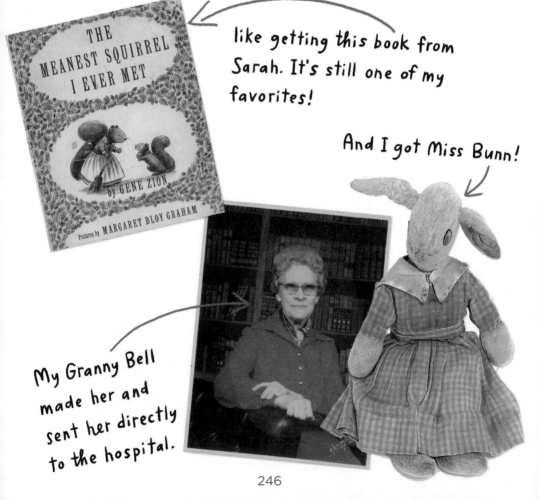

My Granny Bell made her and sent her directly to the hospital.

I was in the hospital for two weeks. Plenty of time to do about a hundred drawings like these. The girl's face was green in every one of them. Maybe I was drawing my illness.

Here are the results of a hearing test that an audiologist gave me. This document (featured on page 17) is called an audiogram. The red circles represent the right ear, and the blue exes represent the left ear. Normal hearing would look like a straight line at the top of the chart. But my lines go down, down, down. The hearing loss for both ears was considered "severe to profound."

J.B. Fisher Elementary
School in Richmond,
Virginia. This is where
Dorn taught me and
my deaf classmates
how to lip-read.

Emma's mom!

Here's me with sweet Emma!
We're sitting on the front
steps of my house in
Richmond. I remember those
awesome bell-bottom pants!

Emma!

We moved into
this big old house
in Salem, Virginia,
in 1976.

Here's me in first grade. Check out the (straps) and the (cords) of the brand-new Phonic Ear underneath my overalls.

My first-grade teacher, "Mrs. Lufton." Her real name is Mrs. Duffy. She is a good sport about being in the book!

A note from my audiologist recommending that I use the Phonic Ear in my new school.

The microphone!

The Phonic Ear!

PHONIC EAR®

ROANOKE COUNTY PUBLIC SCHOOLS

Conference

DATE September 20, 1976

NAME Richard Hawkins
(RVSHC)

PHONE NO.

SCHOOL Academy Street

REFERENCE Cecelia Bell

TOPICS DISCUSSED:
"Cece" has a severe nerve loss bilaterally due to menengitis - in May, 1975.
Mr. Hawkins reports that it is important that she get all possible speech stimulation in the classroom.
An auditory trainer is recommended for use in the classroom and for specific activities in the home.
An FM broadcast unit would be most useful and appropriate. Cost of this system to range between $1,000 - $1,500.
Hawkins will send audiometric reports.
→ Does not appear necessary for her to be in special hearing impaired class - the loss was acquired not congenital. She has good speech, had normal hearing for 5 childhood years. She doesn't consider herself deaf. Putting her in a deaf class would hinder her.

My third-grade school photo. I was always careful to keep the Phonic Ear tucked away under overalls...

and I loved my overalls so much that I wore them even when I wasn't wearing the Phonic Ear.

Granny Bell made these for me. She was amazing!

I became an official member of the Girl Scouts when I was in the second or third grade. That's my friend, Liz. (She's sort of the inspiration for "Carrie" on page 89 in the book.)

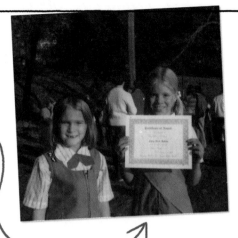

I had many years of speech therapy. I struggled with "s" and "r" sounds. Speech therapy was in a tiny closet under the school stairs, and I hated missing class. My speech therapist wrote to my mom and told her I was not a good sport about speech therapy!

(My mom wrote back and then set me up with a speech therapist outside of school. Thank you, sweet Mama!)

Here's me in the fourth grade, around the time Martha and I became friends.

Martha!

Martha's family

Martha's dad

Martha's mom

Sarah (We both have older sisters named Sarah!)

Catherine

Martha!

Martha and her sisters, Sarah and Catherine.

I am still friends with Martha and her family all these years later!

Martha's house

The dreamy Mike Miller stands on his front porch with his siblings.

Mike moved away when we were in the tenth grade, but we reunited thirty years later. Here we are modeling the Phonic Ear and microphone in San Diego, California. Lots of readers want to know: Did we get married? No, we did not. But we are still friends!

1980: Fifth grade! New glasses! Giant collar!

My fifth grade report card. I got an "E" for "Excellent" in Physical Education. That was when I did the flexed-arm hang for 64 seconds!

NAME _Ceci Bell_

SUBJECT	First Report	Second Report	Third Report	Fourth Report	ACHIEVEMENT FINAL GRADE
Reading	B	B	B	B	B
English	A-	B	B	A	A
Spelling	B	C	B	A	B
Handwriting	B	A	B	A	A
Mathematics	A	A	A	A	A
**Social Science	A-	A	B	A	A
Science	B	A	B+	H	
Health	S	S	E	E	E
Physical Education	S	E	E	E	E
Music	S	S	S	S	S
Art					

**Science, Social Studies and Health

PERFORMANCE CHECK LIST

Key: √ - Continuously
X - Not Consistently
Blank Space - Not Covered

LANGUAGE ARTS
Working at grade level in textbook***
Working below grade level in textbook***

READING
Reads with understanding
Reads well orally
Recognizes and retains basic vocabulary
Uses skills to understand new words
Shows interest in independent reading

ENGLISH
Expresses ideas orally
Applies grammar skills
Uses the dictionary
Applies listening skills
Expresses written ideas clearly

SPELLING
Writes assigned words correctly
Spells correctly in other written work

MATHEMATICS
Working at grade level
Working below grade level
Understands new concepts
Understands basic facts and operations
Uses number skills accurately
Reasons well in problem solving

SOCIAL SCIENCES
Understands and applies new concepts
Takes part in group activities
Contributes to group discussions
Organizes and uses materials

CITIZENSHIP — SOCIAL DEVELOPMENT AND WORK HABITS

1. Is making satisfactory progress
2. Needs to display cooperative attitude
3. Needs to be more attentive
4. Needs to show consideration for others
5. Needs to accept responsibility
6. Needs to complete assignments
7. Needs to listen to and follow directions
8. Needs to work independently
9. Needs to use time wisely
10. Study

EXPLANATION OF MARKS
(See page 3)

A - Superior
B - Above Average
C - Average
D - Below Average
F - Unsatisfactory
Blank Space - Material not covered

E - Excellent
S - Satisfactory
N - Needs Improvement

Physical Education,
Music and Art

PARENT-TEACHER COMMENTS

First Report Period
Ceci has made good progress. She does need to work a little harder on organizing her study materials. We are proud of her progress. S. Suik
Conference requested by parent _____ by teacher
Signature of Parent _Barbara B Bell_

Second Report Period

Conference requested by parent _____ by teacher
Signature of Parent _Barbara B Bell_

Third Report Period

Conference requested by parent _____ by teacher
Signature of Parent _Barbara B Bell_

Fourth Report Period

HOLT, RINEHART AND WINSTON READING TEXTBOOKS

2

My glasses improved my lip-reading
skills, and my grades went up, up, up.

SUBJECT	Achievement / First Report	Citizenship	Achievement / Second Report	Citizenship	Achievement / Third Report	Citizenship	Achievement / Fourth Report	Citizenship	ACHIEVEMENT / FINAL GRADE
Reading	A	1	A	1	A	1	A	1	A
English	A	1	A	1	A	1	A	1	A
Spelling	A	1	A	1	A	1	A	1	A
Handwriting	A	1	A	1	A	1	A	1	A
Mathematics	A	1	A	1	A	1	A	1	A
**Social Studies	A	1	A	1	A	1	A	1	A
Science	A	1	A	1	A	1	A	1	A
Health	A	1	A	1	A	1	A	1	A
Physical Education	S	1	S	1	S	1	S	1	S
Music									
Art	E+	1	E	1	E	1	E	1	E

**Science, Social Studies and Health

CITIZENSHIP — SOCIAL DEVELOPMENT AND WORK HABITS

1. Is making satisfactory progress
2. Needs to display cooperative attitude
3. Needs to be more attentive
4. Needs to show consideration for others
5. Needs to accept responsibility
6. Needs to complete assignments
7. Needs to listen to and follow directions
8. Needs to work independently
9. Needs to use time wisely

EXPLANATION OF MARKS
(See page 5)

A - Superior
B - Above Average
C - Average
D - Below Average
F - Unsatisfactory
Blank Space - Material not covered

E - Excellent
S - Satisfactory
N - Needs Improvement

Physical Education,
Music and Art

PERFORMANCE CHECK LIST

Key: ✓ - Consistently
X - Not Consistently
Blank Space - Not Covered

	REPORT PERIOD			
	1	2	3	4
LANGUAGE ARTS				
Working at grade level in textbook***		✓	✓	✓
Working below grade level in textbook***	✓			
READING				
Reads with understanding	✓	X	✓	✓
Reads well orally	✓	X	✓	✓
Recognizes and retains basic vocabulary	✓	X	✓	✓
Uses skills to understand new words	✓	X	✓	✓
Shows interest in independent reading	✓	✓	✓	
ENGLISH				
Expresses ideas orally		✓	✓	✓
Applies grammar skills		✓	✓	✓
Uses the dictionary		✓	✓	✓
Applies listening skills		✓	✓	✓
Expresses written ideas clearly		✓	✓	✓
SPELLING				
Writes assigned words correctly	✓	✓	✓	✓
Spells correctly in other written work	✓	✓	X	✓
MATHEMATICS				
Working at grade level	✓	✓	✓	✓
Working below grade level				
Understands new concepts	✓		✓	✓
Understands basic facts and operations	✓		✓	✓
Uses number skills accurately	✓		✓	✓
Reasons well in problem solving	✓		✓	✓
SOCIAL SCIENCES				
Understands and applies new concepts		✓	✓	✓
Takes part in group activities		✓	✓	✓
Contributes in group discussions		✓	✓	✓
Organizes and uses materials		✓	✓	✓

HOLT, RINEHART AND WINSTON READING TEXTBOOKS

GRADE LEVEL	***BOOK LEVEL	TITLE
Kindergarten		
Grade 1		About Me (Readiness 1)
		Here, See, Jim, Wyne (Readiness 2)
		Rhymes and Tales (Preprimer 1)
		Books and Games (Preprimer 2)
		Pots and People (Preprimer 3)
		Can You Imagine? (Preprimer 3)
		A Place for Me (Primer)
Grade 2		A Time for Friends (1 Reader)
		People Need People (2¹ Reader)
Grade 3		Never Give Up (3¹ Reader)
		Moon Gets Up (3² Reader)
Grade 4		Special Happenings (4¹ Reader)
Grade 5		Clues To Myself (5th Reader)
Grade 6		Freedom's Ground (6th Reader)
		Riders on the Earth (6th Reader)

PARENT-TEACHER COMMENTS

First Report Period

Conference requested by parent _____ by teacher _____
Signature of Parent *Barbara B. Be*

Second Report Period

Conference requested by parent _____ by teacher _____
Signature of Parent *Barbara B. Be*

Third Report Period

Conference requested by parent _____ by teacher _____
Signature of Parent *Barbara B. Bell*

Fourth Report Period

*It's been a great year!
Let me hear from you.
A. Wilk*

My imaginary self,
El Deafo, really did
help me see myself in
a more positive way.
By the end of fifth
grade, I was a lot
more confident and
a lot less lonely, too.

The idea for the book *El Deafo* began with a blog about my hearing loss. It solidified even more when I created some artwork for a group exhibit. The assignment was to create a postcard that personifies YOU.

These are the sketches and the final postcard for that exhibit.

Here are the first color samples that I sent to my amazing editor, Susan Van Metre.

She really liked what she saw, but suggested I make the artwork look a little bit "older."

So I "aged up" the same artwork a bit, and gave it a darker palette.

It's so green, it looks like El Deafo is underwater!

It helps to have photos that guide your drawings.

My young friend Emily was the perfect size to model my old overalls and the Phonic Ear. She is rocking the look!

Posing like El Deafo!

Mike Miller's STOOP!

Mike Miller's house

I went to first grade here, at Academy Street School...

and then I went to G.W. Carver Elementary School for second through sixth.

I did my flexed-arm hang in this very gym!

G.W. Carver interior

I was using the bathroom during a school visit when I realized that the toilet looked exactly like the old toilets at Carver— so I took a picture!

When I started writing *El Deafo*, I began
with an outline. Each chunk of the outline
became a chapter of the book.

I circled parts of the outline that I could
imagine visually, and then I drew little
tiny pictures to figure out the layouts
and pacing for each page.

El Deafo was my
first graphic novel.
I didn't know what
I was doing.

When I first started
drawing it, I tried to
cram way too many
panels on each page.

12 panels!!

20 panels!!!

Susan advised me
to let the pages
and the storytelling
"breathe" a little,
and so we agreed
to cut back on the
number of panels
per page.

After working on several chapters, I finally got comfortable with a pretty good system. Here's that process from start to finish. I'll focus on the second page of Chapter 11.

Step 1: Reread Chapter 11 outline and divide it up into potential pages.

SUPERCRUSH: The summer after fourth grade, Mike Miller moves into the neighborhood, just two doors down from me. He and his siblings are the most beautiful people I have ever seen. Martha and the other neighborhood kids agree. The teenage girls in the neighborhood adore Mike's big brother. The teenage boys adore Mike's big sister. Little boys adore Mike's little sister. And I adore Mike.

(Secretly... *secretly*! My parents would tease me mercilessly if they *did* know!) He is cute, of course, and I am sure he must be nice, too. I just know in my heart that he wouldn't over-enunciate if he talked to me – but I am too flabbergasted by his cuteness and probable niceness to find out. A Maybe-Friend, perhaps? I could be satisfied with that. A True Friend? I don't dare hope for that. So... cute? Absolutely. Nice? Hopefully. And... trampoline? Yes, indeed – Mike Miller has a trampoline. If we get permission from our parents, we can jump on it. For now, the best I can do is to get Martha to knock on Mike Miller's door, hope that Mike Miller answers it, and then, without actually looking directly at him, ask "Can we jump on your tramp? Our moms said yes!" and then run to his backyard before he has a chance to answer. It is a very bouncy summer.

EL DEAFO Fantasy: Rosette of Beauty entrances Mike Miller! El Deafo to Mike Miller,

SUPERCRUSH: I adore you! (But don't tell anybody!)

① That summer after I meet Martha starts out great!
   [page showing summer activities]
   That is moving in 2 doors down from me.

② And then it gets even better.
   Mike Miller comes to town
   moving van
   each sibling
   w/ adoring neighborhood kids
   (rock star)
   walking to BB
   bare feet on floor of store
   roller skating
   here comes the judge

③ I study MM – become a MM scholar
   w/ notebook
   secret
   Hello? Hello?
   Martha: what are y'... about all moving... the time?
   Peace Corps stuff

④ My love for MM:
   Fantasy or chart – why MM is the perfect boy for me
   an (essay) on MM
   include trampoline
   don't tell M or mom & Dad

   LOVE SCHOLAR

Step 2: Draw small, rough versions of each page, with narration and dialogue on the side.

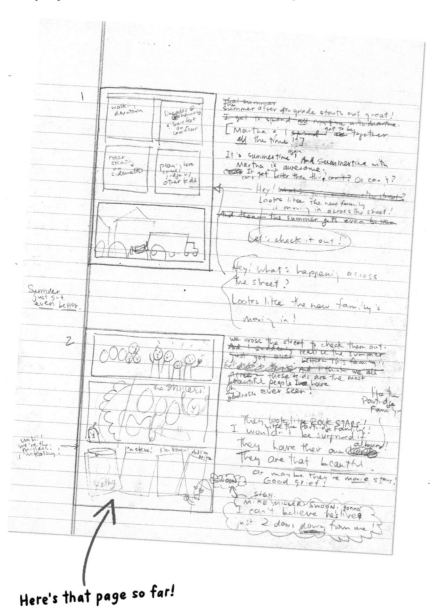

Here's that page so far!

Step 3: The sketch for each page gets bigger and more detailed, and the narration and dialogue really shape up!

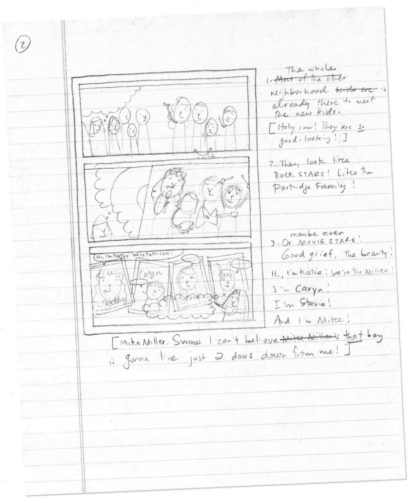

Step 4: I switch from pencil on paper to drawing directly on a Wacom Cintiq tablet hooked up to my computer.

The drawing gets bigger and more detailed.
I type in the narration and dialogue. The fonts
I used for the text are ones that I created
to look like my handwriting.

Step 5: I do the final "inking" using my Wacom tablet and a Photoshop brush. The text is finalized, too.

Step 6: The inked file is sent to the colorist, David Lasky. He adds shadows and colors. The page is complete! Hurrah!

Sometimes it was really difficult to get a page just right. That was the case with page 45.

I made lots of thumbnail drawings like these, trying to get the storytelling and pacing for this page to work.

270

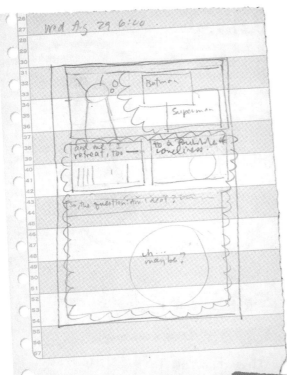

I was haunted by this page. I thought about it all the time, trying to come up with a solution...

and I drew on any scrap of paper I could find...in the car, in the recycling bin, on the ground. You wouldn't know it to look at it, but I finally figured it all out on this old paper bag!

Coloring El Deafo

A David Lasky version of El Deafo!

In the world of comics, it is very common for one person to draw the art, and then for another person to color it. David Lasky was my colorist, and he and I have been friends for thirty years! We both did art for our college newspaper. He is an amazing comics artist.

You can tell from this note to me that he is one of the nicest people you could ever meet.

Dear Cece,

Here's a big batch of shadow drawings I made for "El Deafo"— a behind-the-scenes feature that probably only you and me would have any interest in. I leave the stack with you to decide the fate of.

I do think it was important that I drew the shadows on paper, rather than digitally. It was not easy for me to create new lines within your existing art, and I appreciate that you trusted me to do so.

Some of these I worked on while visiting my mother in Florida. She and Leeann and I drove from Orlando to Gainesville and back, and I drew some of the shadows in the car (at the risk of motion-sickness!).

I'm so proud to have been a part of such a personal book by such a good friend. And I'm glad it's reaching an appreciative audience! Looking forward to seeing you, Tom, Oscar, and Charlie in S.F. in June!

Best wishes,
David

David added all the shadows to the art. (I am not good at shadows!) The shadows really enhance the moods throughout the book.

David's got a great eye for color, too. This was the color palette he created after I sent him some ideas of what I wanted.

You might think that the cover is the first thing that you make for a book, but it often comes last.

I did a lot of variations for the cover. I like how this one looks like an old comic book cover.

This one focuses on the ears and earpieces a lot more.

I tried a mash-up of an old school photo and hand-drawn rabbit ears. Still not quite right!

The designers and I experimented with simpler and more abstract versions.

You might recognize the beginnings of the cursive writing used for the title on the final cover.

El Deafo got a note from
Dogman creator Dav Pilkey...

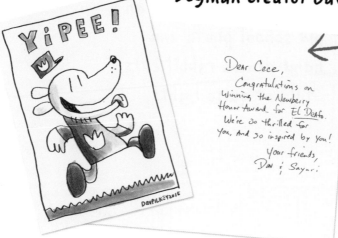

Dear Cece,
Congratulations on
Winning the Newbery
Honor Award for El Deafo.
We're so thrilled for
you. And so inspired by you!
Your friends,
Dav & Sayuri

and an Eisner...

When El Deafo first went out
into the world, I was very
nervous to be sharing my own
story. I could not have
predicted how well it was
received...all over the world!

Foreign editions!

...and a Newbery Honor!

The Association for Library Service to Children,
a division of the American Library Association,

is pleased to recognize

Cece Bell

author of

El Deafo

2015 Newbery Honor Book

Believe it or not, that's
a cake! It was delicious!

Two heads are
better than one:
My editor, Susan
Van Metre, and I
celebrate *El Deafo's*
success.

Dear Cece bell.

Hello, cece

My name is Jabin   . I live in Seoul, Korea.
I go to Jangwon Middle School. But I soon
go to high school. I read your book El Deafo
my school's native English for teacher helped me.
I like reading your book. Your book is fun and
useful for studing English. It is interesting.
My favorite part is CeCe's first love.
In this part, Cece is very cute! hahe. I wanted
more love story! I wonder if Mike In this part,
was your first love. Who is husband? Why did you
draw yourself as a rabbit? Did you not meet
again with Laura again? I have many questions
But. I am not very good at English.
I couldn't understand everything.
But. I like your story!

Dear CeCe Bell,

My name is Hyun-Soo   I live in Seoul, Korea.
I go to Jang-won middle school
I read about your book, "El Deafo".
My favorite part is when your mother believe you didn't
cheat on the test. I wanted to tell your teacher
that you can't see the board?
I've got a similar story.
I wear glasses, too. And before I got glasses,
I couldn't see the board like you.
I got a question for you.
Is it uncomfortable to wear your hearing aid?
Finally, thank you for reading my letter.

Dear CeCe Bell
My name is Ga Eun
I live in Seoul, Korea. I go to Jang won
Middle School.
I read "El Deafo" It's very very good!
My Favorite Part is when You become
friends with Martha. And You Play games
together and have a great time.
I like the way you get along with
each other. By the way I wear glasses
too. I like to listen to music.
How about You? What genre do
You like?

**I truly appreciate how much time
my young readers have spent reading
about El Deafo and thinking about her.**

Dear. Cece Bell

My name is Min-a
I live in seoul, korea. and I go to Jangwon
Middle School.
In My English teacher's Winter Camp, I read EL Deafo.
I think EL Deafo is realistic because I can easily
understand your mind and what it was like to be deaf.
When Ginny speaks too slowly, Cece (You) looks more and more
frustrated. So I understand why you imagined to break ginny's
record.
While reading this book, I felt and thought many things,
like my life in elementary school.
when I was In 5th grade, without even knowing the reason,
three girls blame me and treated me Madly.
because I had a similar experience so I can relate to you.
I really respect you for writing 'EL Deafo'.
oh! Furthermore, you and I wear glasses.
Perhaps we have many things in common.
Lastly, I'm just ask one question.
Do you still have a difficult time these days?
I'm honored to write a letter you as reading this book.
I hope you to see later

From. Min-a

Dear Cece,
I love El Deafo so much.
Thank you for the book and book-
ark! I gave my teacher a copy of the
book and we read it in class. Everone
laughed and they think my hearing aid is
so cool! I an the first one in NM to
have it. (Ponto System) I just got
a streamer for it. My farorite part of
the book is when you hear your teacher
go to the bathroom! El Deafo is th
BEST BOOK EVER! It helps me
be happy and not scared. The
doctor put a setting on my hearing aid
so I can't change the volume and
hear my teacher tinkle tinkle.
Thank you for the Christmas
card I celebrate Chanukah.

Bright holiday wishes to you and yours

January 25, 2018

Dear Cece Bell,

Hi my name is Lucas. I'm in 3rd grade, I also have hearing loss.

The book is funny. I did a book report on El Deafo and I gave it five stars.

I like the part when you wear going crazy over Mike Miller.

Was Laura actually mean and was she real?

thank you

Lucas

Bronx New York!!

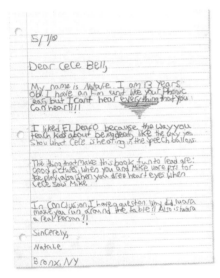

5/7/18

Dear Cece Bell,

My name is Natalie. I am 13 years old. I have an Fm unit like your Phonic ears but I can't hear everything that you can hear!!!

I liked El Deafo because, the way you teach kids about being deaf, like the way you show what Cece is hearing in the speech balloons.

The thing that makes this book fun to read are: good pictures, when you and Mike were pals for the play, also when you drew heart eyes when Cece saw Mike.

In Conclusion, I have a question why did Laura make you run around the table?! Also is Laura a real person?!

SinCerely,

Natalie

Bronx, NY

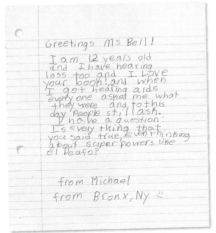

Greetings Ms Bell!

I am 12 years old and I have hearing loss too and I Love your book!, and when I got hearing aids everyone asked me what they were and, to this day, people still ask. I have a question: Is everything that you said true, even thinking about super powers like El Deafo?

from Michael

from Bronx, Ny

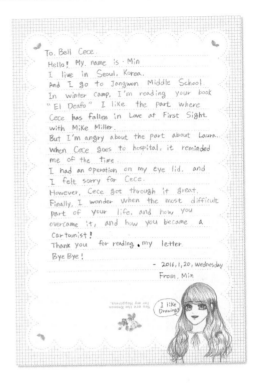

To: Bell Cece.
Hello! My name is Min
I live in Seoul, Korea.
And I go to Jangwon Middle School
In winter camp, I'm reading your book
"El Deafo" I like the part where
Cece has fallen in Love at First Sight
with Mike Miller.
But I'm angry about the part about Laura.
When Cece goes to hospital, it reminded
me of the time.
I had an operation on my eye lid. and
I felt sorry for Cece.
However, Cece got through it great.
Finally, I wonder when the most difficult
part of your life, and how you
overcame it, and how you became a
Cartoonist!
Thank you for reading my letter.
Bye Bye!
                        - 2016, 1, 20, wednesday
                                From, Min

I like
Drawing!

It's wonderful to connect with all of you who get it. We are more alike than we are different!

Dear Cece,
I have read your book "El Deafo"
at least 30 times now. I'm
a BIG fan of you. How did I become
a BIG fan of you? you say? I became
one normal school day I came
home. Then I did my stuff and "KGA!"
my mom pretends that her stomach
was hurting. I knew I was
getting something! I ran to my mom
and I yell "WHAT? WHAT?" And a book
ploped out from under her shirt.
I quickly grabed the book and ran
to my room. I read the Title.
"El Deafo Eh? "I can wait!" I
Quickly read it "I LOVE IT!" SO
That's how I'm a fan!
How Long did it take you
to make your Book?
also what is your
favorite Color?!

LOVE U!
your Fan
Link

I love my readers

Comic book by Blair and his students at the Free Union Country School

El Deafo's fans are amazing artists, too! I've received some wonderful artwork, like a hand-drawn comic book from a teacher and his students...

as well as terrific representations of El Deafo in all sorts of media!

Crochet by Yumi

Colored pencil by Neomi

Envelope art by Linka

Ballpoint pen by Sophia

Felt and embroidery by Camille and Lucia

You are all amazing!

Thank you so much for reading my book.
I hope you enjoyed these little extras
and that they will inspire you to share
YOUR story.

xoxo
Cece Bell

Pen-and-ink by Joe Sutphin

Ink brush by Lunch Lady
creator Jarrett Krosoczka

Crayon

Cece Bell has written and illustrated several books for children, including the Geisel Honor book *Rabbit & Robot: The Sleepover* and *Chick and Brain: Smell My Foot!* She lives in Virginia with her husband, Tom Angleberger.